THE BRIDGE BATTLE

NPL | F

Nashville Public Library | FOUNDATION

THE BRIDGE BATTLE

JACQUELINE DAVIES

Clarion Books
An Imprint of HarperCollins*Publishers*

Special thanks to Professor John Ochsendorf from the
Department of Civil and Environmental Engineering at MIT for
reviewing the material on bridge structure and the concepts
of tension and compression.

Clarion Books is an imprint of HarperCollins Publishers.

Bridge Battle
Copyright © 2022 by Jacqueline Davies
Illustrations by Cara Llewellyn

ISBN 978-0-35-869299-7

Typography by Alice Wang
The artist used pen and ink to create the illustrations for this book.
22 23 24 25 26   PC/LSCC   10 9 8 7 6 5 4 3 2 1
❖
First Edition

For Joy Bernstein and Charlie Rich,
good neighbors and
true patrons of the arts

CONTENTS

CHAPTER 1
WELCOME TO FAIRY LAND

"Geese!" said Jessie, wrinkling her nose and pointing at a pair of birds nibbling grass on the playground. "I don't like geese."

"I know," said her mother, hurrying up the path
to the school. They were almost—but not quite—
late for the first day of Summer Fun Exploration
Camp. "Just stay away from them, okay?"

"Are you *kidding* me? I wouldn't get within fifty
feet of those geese!" said Jessie indignantly. "Do you
know how much they poop?"

"No," said Mrs. Treski.

"Well, I do!" said Jessie, breaking into a run. Jessie was small for her age and often had to jog to keep up with her mother and older brother, Evan. Her backpack, heavy with its special book inside, banged against her rear end with every step.

"I thought you would," said Mrs. Treski, scanning the playground. All the other kids had gone inside. They were definitely late.

"A Canada goose makes up to two pounds of poop *every day!*"

"Jessie, please," said her mother. "We need to find your class."

Jessie stopped on the walkway and folded both her arms across her chest. "*My* class was Young Engineers: Build Your Own Bridges!" she said. "*That's* the one I signed up for."

"I know," said Mrs. Treski. "It's my fault. I sent in the form late. I'm sorry, Jess. But you can still have fun in a different class."

"How to Make and Decorate *Fairy Houses?*" shouted Jessie. "Are you *kidding* me?" Jessie still couldn't believe that she had to spend three whole weeks doing something as ridiculous, as foolish, as *dishonest* as making fairy houses. *There are no such thing as fairies.* Jessie was nine years old and she knew this for a fact. She had *never* believed in fairies. Never.

Before this morning, Jessie had hoped the class would be canceled. She was the sixth person to sign up for the class, and there had to be at least *seven* students or the class would be canceled. For two weeks, Jessie had waited to get the cancellation email. It never came.

"It'll be fun," said Mrs. Treski, trying to open the side door of the school. It was locked. They would have to climb the hill, for which the school was named, and enter through the front door.

Jessie was about to list all the ways that this fairy class would *not* be fun—she could think of at least eight reasons right off the top of her head—when she caught sight of her mother's face. Her mother's lips were pressed together, her cheeks were red, and her eyebrows dipped down at the sides.

Jessie knew from her emotions flash cards that these three things meant that her mother was "worried" or "frustrated." Why would her mother be worried or frustrated? Jessie wondered. *She* wasn't the one who was going to be stuck at Summer Fun Exploration Camp building fairy houses for three weeks!

Jessie checked her mother's face again. Feelings were often a mystery to Jessie. Still, she was getting better at reading the clues on people's faces. And she didn't want to make her mom feel worse. Jessie knew it was hard being a grownup and taking care of two kids all on her own. Evan had explained that to her. Evan explained a lot of things to Jessie.

She hitched up her backpack on her shoulders and started to walk up the hill. One of the geese on the playground flapped its wings and honked loudly, causing Jessie to look toward the stream and the middle school beyond.

"Look!" shouted Jessie, pointing across the playground fields. "I see Evan!"

Mrs. Treski stopped and looked beyond the little

stream that separated the elementary school and the town's one middle school. Jessie shouted, "Hey! Evan! Over here!"

Evan was starting his first day of summer school. Summer school was *not* the same as Summer Fun Exploration Camp. Evan had told her this, too. It was *real* school for kids who needed extra help. Jessie had wanted Evan to walk to camp with her, but he had said, "No way! I'm not showing up on the first day of school with my little sister!" Jessie wished she was going to real school instead of camp. In fact, she would rather sit on a mound of dirt filled with ten thousand biting fire ants than spend three weeks building fairy houses.

Evan looked in her direction. There were other kids entering the middle school. He didn't wave to her. Instead, he hunched his shoulders and kept on walking toward the school entrance.

Jessie frowned.

"C'mon, Jess," said her mother, tugging gently on Jessie's backpack because Jessie didn't like to be touched.

"Mom, I know the way," said Jessie. "You don't have to walk me in." This was the school that she and Evan went to. Next year, they would both be in the fifth grade, even though Jessie was a year younger than Evan. She had skipped third grade because she was "academically advanced." And also because those three horrible girls—Lorelei, Andrea, and most especially Becky Baker—had played a really mean trick on her. If she had had her way, she would have sent all three of them to live in a different town—perhaps one with *lots* of mounds of dirt filled with fire ants.

But no one had been sent away. Instead, the three girls had gone to the principal's office and Jessie had gotten to skip ahead to Evan's grade. She was glad to be away from those girls forever.

"Okay," said Mrs. Treski. "I have a meeting that starts in ten minutes. You'll be fine." She knelt down so she was looking right into Jessie's face. "Look. I know this isn't what you wanted. But try to make the best of it, okay?"

"Lemons into lemonade," said Jessie glumly.

"Exactly. We're Treskis. We know how to roll with the punches, right?"

Jessie nodded, but inside she was thinking, *Three weeks!* She looked across the field to the middle school. The stream with the marshlands in between the two schools was a stopping-off point for migrating Canada geese and a permanent home for the ones that didn't migrate. Every year a few pairs made their nests in the tall grasses near the stream. All the kids at Hillside Elementary thought the goslings that hatched were cute, but Jessie knew that those cute babies would grow into adult geese that made even more poop! She was *not* a fan of baby geese.

Jessie entered the school and walked straight to the art room, a room she had never liked because the art teacher kept it very messy. The scissors were never in the right place, the glue bottles had gunky dried bits crusted on the tips, the floor was littered with hard blobs of clay, and the paper wasn't sorted by color, starting with red and ending with violet, the way the light spectrum sorted colors. If Jessie had her way, she would reorganize the entire art room. Jessie liked to organize.

But when she walked into the art room this morning, it was almost empty. All the art supplies had been removed for the summer, and the long black tables had been scrubbed down so that they were completely smooth. Even the walls were bare. Jessie liked it!

"Hello! And welcome," said a young woman dressed in a fairy costume. She didn't look old enough to be a teacher, but she was definitely too old to be dressed like a fairy. She had a sparkly silver sequined top and a puffy tulle skirt like a ballerina. She was also wearing a glittery diamond tiara on top of her jet-black hair, and dangly diamond earrings that were so long they brushed the tops of her bare shoulders. Jessie counted six earrings—in each ear! The gossamer fairy wings on her back twinkled, as did her shimmering nose ring. In one hand, she held a star wand made from a striped drinking straw and in the other she held a pinch of silver glitter. There was a colorful tattoo on her wrist of a seagull standing on a rock. She twirled toward Jessie, did a kitty-cat leap, and tossed some glitter into the air. "Welcome to Fairy Land!" she said.

"Stop it!" shouted Jessie, trying to swipe the glitter away. Jessie *hated* glitter. It was messy and fake and you could never get rid of it, no matter how hard you tried. It stuck and it stuck and it stuck, and days after cleaning it up, you would still find bits of it on the floor or on your cheek or in your bed. Jessie's best friend, Megan, loved glitter, but even when Megan had used it to decorate their lemonade stand last summer, Jessie had refused to touch it.

"Sorry! *Um.* Are you okay? Good. Ha! That was a mistake. My name is Pixie Fairydust!" said the teacher. "I'm so glad you'll be part of our Fairy Circle!" She picked up an ordinary clipboard and asked, "What is your name, please?"

A girl's voice from the other end of the room answered, "Freak," followed by a shower of laughter.

Jessie felt her cheeks get hot. She looked over. There were five girls of different ages seated at one of the long black art tables. Her eyes quickly spotted a cluster of three at one end who bent their heads together like flowers after a rain.

There was Lorelei.

There was Andrea.

And there was Becky Baker.

All three were sitting on stools, leaning their elbows on one of the smooth, clean art tables. All three were smiling as if they were the nicest girls in the world. But Jessie knew the truth. They were not nice girls. They were poison.

Becky Baker. This was going to be the worst Summer Fun Exploration Camp ever.

CHAPTER 2

NATURAL-BORN LEADER

Evan approached the middle school slowly. He had been inside it before. Basketball practices for the town-wide teams were sometimes held in the middle school gym. Still, it wasn't his turf, and he could feel it, so he approached cautiously, his eyes scanning to see if he knew any of the boys, noticing who was standing with whom, trying to guess the ages of the kids, hoping to spot just one familiar face.

Evan reminded himself he was good at this. It was easy for him to talk to people. When he and his mom and Jessie went to the beach, Evan always found kids to play Frisbee with, while Jessie was happy to collect shells in a bucket or sit by herself reading.

Everyone liked Evan. He was good at getting along. On all his report cards, his teachers would write: "Well liked. Works well in groups. A natural-born leader."

But they also wrote things like: "Needs academic support. Would benefit from extra help in reading fundamentals. Not up to grade level in math."

His fourth grade teacher had strongly recommended summer school, and that had sealed his fate. This summer, he would be in school every day for eight weeks. None of his friends had to go. Only him. He felt like he was being sent into the desert with a lame camel and a half-empty canteen.

"Hey," he said to the one boy who sat by himself at a picnic table. "My name's Evan."

The boy, whose back was to Evan, quickly scooped something off the picnic table and stuffed it in his pocket. When he turned around, Evan saw that the boy was small, with rectangular glasses that seemed too big for him, and a large birthmark on his left cheek. His hair was cut badly so that he had a serious spike right at the crown of his head.

The boy looked at him, then over at the larger group of boys standing in the middle of the black-top. He squinted into the sun, and the light bounced off his glasses, creating so much glare that it looked to Evan like he had no eyes at all.

"Are you friends with them?" the boy asked. He curled his fingers under so that the tips pressed against the palms of his hands. Close and open. Close and open. Evan noticed that one of the boy's front teeth was slightly chipped.

Evan looked over at the boys too. They were his height or even taller. The biggest one was leaning against a basketball pole, with one foot propped up against it. The other boys were turned toward him.

Evan understood this. A group is like a wheel, and the tall boy was at the center. He was the hub, and the others were just spokes that radiated off him.

"Nah," Evan said to the boy. "I don't know any of them. Do you think they're in elementary school, like us?"

The boy straightened up, anger flashing across his face. "I'm going into seventh grade next year," he said. "What grade are *you* in?"

Evan flushed. Now he'd said the wrong thing, and he barely even knew this kid. Plus, he had to admit that he was younger. Not a good way to start. "Sorry," said Evan. "I guess I just figured everyone in this class would be in the same grade. I don't know why." He shrugged. "I'm going into fifth grade."

He reached down and scooped up some pebbles, then did a fadeaway jump shot, tossing the pebbles into the air so that they rained down on the blacktop. When Evan needed to think or calm himself down, he always reached for a ball. He wished he'd brought his basketball today. But looking at the older boys, he had second thoughts. *They* weren't playing ball. Maybe it was better just to do nothing. Maybe that's what older kids did on the playground before school.

"You're big for your age," said the other boy, and Evan bit his tongue to keep from saying the obvious: *You're small for yours.*

"Yeah," said Evan, "I'm the tallest kid in my class at Hillside." He pointed to the elementary school across the stream, then scooped up a few more pebbles and started juggling them in the air, tossing them from one palm to the other.

"I wish I was tall," said the boy.

"Well, everybody's got something," said Evan. That's what his mom always said. She meant it both ways: everybody's got talents and everybody's got troubles. She said it to Evan and she said it to Jessie, and she meant it just the same with both.

The boy jammed his hand in his jacket pocket and clutched whatever he had shoved in there a moment earlier. He seemed to be trying to decide something.

"Hey, Jump Shot," shouted a voice across the

blacktop. Evan turned. It was the tall boy, the one who was the center of the wheel. He was still leaning against the basketball pole, as if getting Evan's attention wasn't even worth the trouble of moving.

"Hi," said Evan, smiling. Maybe someone in the group had a ball. Maybe they could shoot a few hoops before going in for their first day of summer school. That would make Evan feel better. Less nervous.

The boy sitting at the picnic table turned away quickly, like a clam snapping shut, so that his back was to Evan and the boys. Evan looked at the boy then drifted a little closer to the circle around the basketball pole. He still had a few pebbles in his hand.

"Bet you can't make a basket with one of those pebbles from—" The tall boy glanced around the blacktop and then pointed. "That line."

Evan smiled. He could make that shot. Maybe tomorrow he could bring his ball and they could start a game in the cool of the morning.

Evan moved up to the line, inching his toes to the very edge of the white paint. He picked the pebble in his hand that had the most weight and the roundest shape. He wished he could dribble it a few times to get his legs under him, but that wouldn't work with a pebble. So he bent his knees twice and then let the pebble sail through the air.

It went right through the net. Dead center. *Everybody's got something,* he thought to himself with satisfaction.

The boys roared, and a few of them even cursed loudly, which surprised Evan since they were so close to the school and a teacher might hear. The biggest kid said, "You're pretty good," and Evan could tell he had won his approval. Maybe summer school wasn't going to be so bad after all. He could make new friends and even hang out with some seventh grade boys. That sounded pretty cool.

The tallest boy sauntered over and draped an arm around Evan's neck. All the other boys trailed behind. "You know how to shoot," he said, tightening his arm in a way that hurt Evan's neck.

Evan smiled and let himself be pushed around a little. It was all in good fun.

Then the tall boy leaned in closer and said, "Do you think you can make that shot?" He pointed to a different part of the playground. But there was no basketball pole there. There was just the picnic table with the boy sitting at it, his back still turned to the other boys.

"What do you mean?" asked Evan.

"See if you can hit him with a pebble from here. It's thirty feet, at least. If you can make that, you're the champ."

"N-o-o-o," said Evan. "I'm not going to do that."

"Aw, c'mon," said the boy. "It's just a pebble. It's not going to hurt him. Look." The tall boy scooped up a pebble, tossed it into the air, and let it land on his own head. "See. It's nothing."

Evan was still holding one pebble in his hand. He couldn't imagine throwing it at some kid's back, a kid he didn't even know. It was different when you were horsing around with your friends. Over the years, he and Paul and Adam had thrown just about everything at each other: wads of paper, superballs, paper clips, even shoes. But Evan didn't do that when a kid had his back turned. That wasn't right.

Suddenly, a pebble flew through the air toward the picnic table. It missed its mark by more than ten feet. Evan didn't know who had thrown it.

The tall boy called out, "Hey, Albert! You're the hoop!" And then all at once the boys were raining jump shots down in the boy's direction. Pebbles flew through the air, and some of them landed on the boy. He tried to cover himself with both hands, cowering lower over the picnic table and smashing down the spike of hair on the top of his head. Evan was frozen where he stood, in the very middle of it all, but feeling a million miles away.

The bell rang, and the boys' joyousness drained away instantly. The tall boy who had put his arm around Evan's neck gave Evan a parting whack on the shoulder. "You missed your shot, bud," he said as the group drifted toward the door.

The boy stood up from the picnic table and shook out his jacket, careful to protect whatever was in his pocket. Some of the pebbles had made their way down his pants, and he tried to shake them out without looking too ridiculous. He kept his back to Evan.

Evan didn't know what to do. He wanted to tell the kid that he hadn't thrown a single pebble, but he knew that that wasn't really the point. Sometimes it's not what you do but what you don't do that makes the difference. And Evan knew that the boy wanted to forget what had just happened, as quickly as possible. Bringing it up now would make it worse.

The boy started toward the school and Evan followed behind, miserable. From far away he heard someone call his name, and he looked up to see Jessie, across the stream at their elementary school. It felt to Evan as if she was in a different universe. He didn't stop to wave.

When Evan and the boy reached the door, Evan

said, "Hey, you didn't tell me your name was Albert. Like I said, I'm Evan." He reached out his hand to shake, the way his mother had taught him to do, but the boy didn't reach back.

"My name *isn't* Albert," said the boy with real anger in his voice. "My name is Stevie. Stupid Stevie. *Albert* is short for Albert Einstein. You watch. He'll give you a nickname too." Then he walked in ahead of Evan and disappeared down the hall.

CHAPTER 3
THE GREAT BIG BOOK OF BRIDGES

Jessie sat by herself at an empty art table, looking at those mean girls and thinking, *This never would have happened if I'd gotten into that bridge-building class.* Jessie felt her stomach flip then flop. What was going to happen?

She stared at the girls. Becky was in the middle, and the other two had their eyes glued on her. They listened to every word she said; they watched every move she made. Sometimes, they copied a gesture of hers.

But then Becky would ignore both of them. Or ignore just one. When she did that, the one who was being ignored would talk louder or sit up taller or put a hand on Becky's arm to make her look at her. Jessie found it all very confusing.

"My grandparents gave it to me for my birthday," said Becky, playing with a long necklace she wore. "They said, so I would always remember them." The necklace had a heavy pendant on a long silver chain. The pendant was made of rose quartz. Jessie knew this because she'd been obsessed with rocks when she was five years old. Even though she no longer collected them, she still had a crystal geode on her night table and could identify a lot of minerals on sight.

She stared at the necklace. What was the shape of the pendant? It reminded Jessie of something. Something she had seen in a book. It was almost like a slice of deep-dish pizza with the tip cut off. Jessie carefully drew the shape of the pendant in her notebook.

Becky's
necklace

long
silver
chain

rose
quartz
stone

"Can I see it?" asked Lorelei, reaching one hand toward Becky's neck.

"No!" Becky jerked the necklace away from Lorelei's hand. "It's very special to me. And *very* expensive, because the stone is so rare. If something happened to it, I would just die."

Jessie knew that it was basically impossible for Lorelei to hurt the pendant, because quartz is one of the strongest minerals on earth and has an extremely high melting point. And quartz was *not* rare. It was the second most common mineral on earth (after feldspar). Jessie wanted to correct Becky, to give her the right facts, but she remembered what Evan had told her about these girls in second grade: they were not nice. Jessie hadn't understood that at the time, but Evan had explained it to her. She kept her mouth closed, although she had to pinch herself to do it.

"I suppose we should get started," said Pixie Fairydust, "even though we have one more coming. So . . ." She looked at the students, and Jessie got that lurchy feeling in her stomach when she knew that something was not in the correct place. Like when her stapler was on the left side of her desk instead of the right. "So-o-o . . . I already said: My name is Pixie Fairydust, and—"

"That's a really weird name!" said Lorelei. She looked at Becky, and Jessie wondered if Lorelei was trying to impress her. Why would saying *that* impress anyone?

"Well, that's my name! Fairies, you know, aren't afraid of being different. They're not afraid of anything!" sang Pixie, a little too brightly. "We have *three* magical weeks together, and during that time you will each make *three* magical fairy houses to take home and keep forever! Let's start by singing a song together. I have my special fairy lute." Pixie grabbed a pink ukulele from behind her teacher's desk and began to strum. The ukulele had several Barbie stickers covering it. Jessie noticed that Pixie's purple nail polish was badly chipped.

Jessie was not interested in a fairy song. She reached into her backpack and took out her special book. She was planning to enter a statewide bridge-building contest. There were different age groups and special categories. Jessie already knew the prize she wanted to win: "Most Innovative, 9–12 Years Old." She hoped the student who was late would never show up and she could spend the whole day reading her book and drawing her designs.

The book was called *The Great Big Book of Bridges*, and it was filled with photographs of bridges all over the world. There were also diagrams that showed how to build working models of bridges. According to the book, you could make bridges out of straws or Popsicle sticks or clay or pencils! All kinds of bridges: arch bridges like the ancient Romans built, and suspension bridges like the Brooklyn Bridge in New York, and double cantilever bridges like the famous Dinosaur Bridge in Japan. There were so many different ways to build a bridge. How many ways could there be to build a fairy house?

"Oops! Sorry!" said Becky. She had gotten up to refill her water bottle at the sink, and on the way back to her seat, she spilled water onto Jessie's book.

"This is a rare book!" said Jessie loudly, which was true because they had found it in the bargain bin at the Friends of the Library book sale, and it was the only one of its kind. The girls laughed at Jessie. She wiped the droplets of water off the glossy page and looked to the teacher to report this misbehavior. But Pixie had finished her song and was in the hallway, waiting for the final student to arrive.

"Who brings a book to summer camp?" asked Andrea, rolling her eyes. Her voice was filled with that sound that Jessie never understood—the one that meant a person was *saying* one thing but meant something else.

"I do," said Jessie, matter-of-factly, and for some reason that made the three girls laugh even more. They laughed so much that Pixie poked her head in the door to see what was going on.

Jessie turned her back on the girls and focused on the photograph of the Lake Pontchartrain Causeway bridge in Louisiana, which was the longest bridge in the world. She liked things that were the *most* of anything: the longest, the strongest, the smartest, the fastest. It was a simple beam bridge, but it stretched twenty-four miles from one end to the other! Jessie drew a picture of the bridge in her notebook.

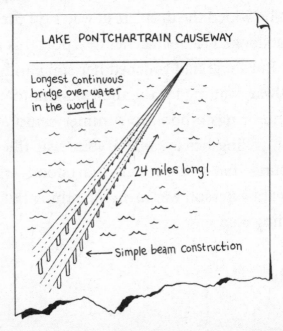

LAKE PONTCHARTRAIN CAUSEWAY

Longest continuous bridge over water in the <u>world</u> !

24 miles long!

Simple beam construction

"Here comes our last student!" sang Pixie from the hallway. Jessie looked up from her notebook just in time to see the very last person she ever expected to walk into a class on building fairy houses.

"David Kirkorian!" said Jessie. "What are *you* doing here?"

David K. was one of the boys who had been in Jessie's fourth grade class, the same class she'd been in with Evan. It was rumored that David collected strange things, like human toenail clippings and the hair from every haircut he'd ever had, but Jessie didn't believe that. Why would anyone collect those things? Then again, when it came to people, a lot of things didn't make sense to Jessie. Why did they smile when they were being mean? Why did they say one thing when they meant exactly the opposite? Why didn't they *all* want to spend the summer building bridges? And why wouldn't they let a friend touch a necklace made out of quartz if the friend wanted to?

David Kirkorian. How much worse could this day get? First, pooping geese. Then those mean girls.

And now David K. It was already embarrassing enough that she was in a class with a teacher named Pixie who seemed to believe she was a fairy. Jessie was ready to pack up her special book and head home.

"Hi!" said David, walking over to Jessie and sitting down next to her. Andrea, Lorelei, and Becky giggled viciously. Jessie scowled.

"Why are you here?" she whispered. "This is not a class for fourth-graders!"

"Technically, we're fifth-graders now," said David with a big grin.

"That makes it even worse!" said Jessie. "This is a baby class." The mean girls had just finished third grade, and Jessie knew that one of the other two girls, Katrina, was just out of kindergarten because she had been Megan's kindergarten buddy. Jessie felt the tips of her ears get hot with the embarrassment of it all.

"I thought it would be fun to build houses," said David.

"Fairy houses!" said Jessie, practically spitting the words.

"Anyway, I heard you telling Megan on the last day of school that you were doing this camp class, so I thought I'd give it a try."

"You!" said Jessie. "You're the last one who signed up? If it weren't for you, I'd be home building bridges right now!"

David sat still. "That statement makes no sense."

"We're all here!" sang Pixie, "so now the fun can begin. Come on, everyone. Let's form our Fairy Circle and get ourselves moving!" She played some twinkly music from her iPhone. It had a lot of harps and zithers, and a steady drumbeat to keep them stepping around the circle in time.

Jessie refused to leave her stool. But Katrina hopped and skipped and twirled as she moved, flapping her arms as if she were flying.

"Why aren't you dancing, Jessie?" asked Katrina as she flapped by. "We're all fairies, and we should dance."

"I am *not* a fairy!" said Jessie. "I'm an engineer."

"An *en-ja*-what?" asked Katrina.

"An *engineer*. It's someone who designs and builds things."

"Like fairy houses!" shouted Katrina gleefully. "I'm an *en-ja*-what, too!" She twirled and then did a series of ninja kicks.

"No!" said Jessie. "Engineers build real things. Like roads and skyscrapers and bridges and dams."

"She said 'dam'! She said 'dam'!" shouted Ava, the other young student in the class. "She's not allowed to say that word."

Pixie raised her arms. "Okay, everybody just calm down. Jessie did not say a bad word."

"Dam! Dam! Dam!" shouted Ava. Jessie could tell that this was Ava's one chance to say that word, and she was going to say it as much as she possibly could.

"Stop!" shouted Pixie, her voice loud enough to drown out all the twinkly harp and zither music. She ran to the classroom door and closed it. "Just everybody CALM DOWN. Okay?"

Jessie leaned forward and whispered to Katrina, who was twirling in front of her. "I came here to *build bridges*."

"Fairy bridges?" asked Katrina, whispering too.

"No," said Jessie, "*real* bridges. Real bridges that can hold weight and transport loads. I'm entering a contest. And I'm going to win!"

Pixie clapped her hands and turned off the music on her phone. "Today we are going to begin by making magic fairy wands! Magical, sparkly wands. Everyone gather at this table and I'll show you how."

Jessie laid her head down on the table. "Oh, brother!" And she meant just that. Why couldn't she be home with Evan? They could be building all kinds of things if they were together for the summer.

"C'mon, Jess," said David. "Let's see who can build the longest wand that doesn't break. I bet I can make one that's six feet long."

That got Jessie going. How long could a wand be? What was the best material for sticking the straws together? How could she reinforce her wand?

"Sorry again!" said Becky, interrupting Jessie's calculations as she knocked over the small bowl of glue in the middle of the table. The sticky white stuff ran all over Jessie's work area.

"You did that on purpose!" said Jessie.

"I did not!" said Becky. "It was an accident." But seconds later Jessie heard Becky whisper to Andrea and Lorelei. The other two girls laughed.

"Here," said David to Jessie. He handed her a dry paper towel. Then he picked up a whole handful of glue-soaked brushes to take to the sink, and as he turned he accidentally flicked a glob of glue in Becky's hair.

"Oh, you idiot!" she shouted. "You got glue in my HAIR!"

"I was just trying to clean up the mess you made," David explained.

Then he looked at Jessie and winked. *What does that mean?* wondered Jessie. She was never sure when people used their faces to send signals.

But Jessie was happy that Becky's long, pretty hair had a big glob of glue in it. And the glob was getting globbier by the minute as Becky tried to wipe it away.

"What's going on here?" asked Pixie, who had been helping Katrina and Ava at the other end of the table. "Oh, Becky! No! You're just making it worse!" Pixie led Becky to the sink. As they passed, Becky turned and stuck out her tongue at Jessie.

Even Jessie knew what *that* signal meant.

CHAPTER 4
GLITCH

Evan soon learned that the tall kid who had draped his arm around Evan's neck was named Reed, and no one called him anything but that. Reed, however, gave nicknames to everyone else. Puke, Li'l Snot, Bunny Butt, Twitch, and Frank, which Evan learned was short for Frankenstein. And, of course, Albert, because Reed thought it was funny to point out that Stevie was no Albert Einstein.

Well, none of us are, thought Evan. *That's why we're in summer school.*

For the moment, Evan's nickname was Jump Shot, but he had a feeling that wouldn't last. Say the wrong thing, do the wrong thing, and suddenly he'd be known as Stinkhead or Pus. As if the eight weeks of summer school weren't already long enough! He didn't need to go around with a nickname like that. No thank you.

During the morning math assessment work-sheet, his mind wandered. He tapped the eraser end of his pencil on the paper and then on his cheek and then on his paper and then on his cheek. Cautiously, he looked around the room. Most of the kids were older, much older, which was strange, because Evan was used to being the tallest one in class.

"Do your work—" Mrs. Warner glanced down at her seating assignment chart. "Evan."

Suddenly, Evan realized that no one knew him here. Not the teachers, the kids, the principal, the nurse, the cafeteria ladies, or even the custodian. At Hillside, *everyone* knew him. Did that mean he was the same person? Or could he be someone else?

Act differently. Talk differently. Wear different clothes. Have a different name. Would he be the same Evan this summer or a different one? And who would know the difference?

Evan could smell the disinfectant that the custodians had sprayed on the desks to wash away a year's worth of germs. It was one of those smells that made him think of vomit, because it's what the custodians used whenever a kid threw up in class. Thinking of vomit made Evan start to feel like maybe he was going to vomit. But then he thought that if he did *that*, he would instantly get a new nickname from Reed, and it would be a whole lot worse than Jump Shot.

"Albert! Hey, Albert!" A voice hissed in a whisper just loud enough to be heard by the other students, but not by Mrs. Warner, who was now talking to another teacher who had just walked into the room.

Evan didn't turn around; he kept his eyes on his paper. So did Stevie. But the voice didn't stop, as Evan knew it wouldn't. *"Hey! Hey! Albie!"* Stevie's eyes drifted up to look at the teachers, who were having a quiet argument. Evan felt as if he could read Stevie's mind. *Do something!* he was trying to tell the teachers.

"Hey! Incoming!"

A red gummy bear flew through the air, but missed Stevie by a few feet. Evan felt his temperature rise. He stared hard at the gummy bear on the floor. It lay on its side, stiff and unmoving, like a pilot shot out of the sky. Stevie didn't turn around, but Evan saw his shoulders tense up.

Then a green gummy bear went flying, and this one hit the back of Stevie's head. He flinched and swiped at his neck, but the gummy bear had already fallen to the floor. Another soldier down in battle.

The teachers moved to a far corner of the room as their voices grew louder in disagreement. They didn't notice what was happening with the attack. Of course, kids like Reed were good at knowing when teachers were distracted. They had a sixth sense for it. Gummy bears. Ingenious. They didn't make a sound when they landed.

Stevie bent his head lower, his shoulders hunched forward, like he was building a small fort around himself.

"Time's up!" said Mrs. Warner loudly. "Put your pencils down and hand your papers forward. Thank you! Thank you!"

Evan had barely made it through half of the questions. Some of it was math stuff he had never even heard of. Factoring? Prime numbers? And what the heck was the associative property? Evan was pretty sure Mrs. Overton had never talked about any of that in fourth grade.

The second teacher, the one who had been disagreeing with Mrs. Warner, came to his desk and said, "Hi, Evan. My name is Miss Dixon. Why don't you come with me?"

Evan didn't like being singled out like this. He knew it made him more of a target for kids like Reed. But he was also glad to get away. He didn't want to watch any more gummy bears flying to their death.

The hallway was long and bleak. No artwork, no posters encouraging good behavior, no doors decorated to look like the covers of books. If this was what middle school was going to be like, it looked pretty grim.

"Here we are," said Miss Dixon. "My secret lair." She smiled wickedly.

They sat down in the cramped room that wasn't much bigger than a closet, side by side at a small rectangular table with a walnut-brown laminate top. Miss Dixon had all her materials laid out on the table: a notebook, three pencils, and a metal board covered with magnetic tiles. The tiles had letters on them, but they were arranged in a way Evan couldn't make any sense of. Evan felt bad for Miss Dixon, stuck in this dreary, windowless room all day. He hoped she got to go outside at least to supervise recess.

"So, Evan," said Miss Dixon. "Here's the thing, and I think you should know it right off the bat." She paused, as if remembering the intense conversation with Mrs. Warner. "You're not supposed to be here. Somehow your name got put in with the middle school kids. We have a new clerk in the office . . ." She shook her head. "That doesn't matter. The students who are still in elementary school— even the ones who have finished fifth grade but haven't started sixth grade yet—are all at Mitchell for the summer."

"Oh," said Evan. "Does that mean I'll take a bus in the morning?" He knew that the Mitchell school was too far to walk, and it would be hard for his mom to handle the dropoff and pickup for both Jessie and him if they were at two different schools on two different schedules. She had to work every day, and time was always tight.

"No," said Miss Dixon. "There aren't buses for the summer session. We can't— It's not that simple. A lot of what summer school is all about is getting one-on-one help with specialists who teach certain very specialized programs: reading specialists, like me, and math interventionists and OT and PT and all kinds of different support teachers. And all our schedules are set for the summer. So even though you'll spend some of the time in the classroom with Mrs. Warner working on general skills, you'll also meet with me every day for reading and Mr. Gee for math review. And because our schedules are already locked in, we can't switch you to Mitchell, which is where you really belong. With kids your own age. Do you see what I mean?"

Evan nodded. A mistake. A glitch. A missed shot. That happened sometimes in basketball, even if you practiced really hard.

"Do you think you'll be okay with that?" asked Miss Dixon seriously. "Being with older kids? It can be hard, especially when you're the only one who's younger. I mean, I know you're tall for your age, so you look like you fit in, but maybe it still feels a little—weird? Uncomfortable?"

Evan looked at Miss Dixon. She seemed like one of the good ones. Hadn't she already said that the teachers' schedules were locked in? And that there were no buses to help his mom get him to the other school? That there was no way a change could be made? He started to get that feeling he sometimes got with his mom, where he could tell he needed to take some of the burden off her shoulders. She worked really hard and had two kids to take care of—and Jessie could be a real pain in the neck sometimes! Evan often felt like he had to tell his mom that things were all right when they weren't. That's what had led to the whole Lemonade War last summer.

"It's no big deal," Evan said, shrugging his shoulders. He was good at being the easy kid. He could take one for the team. "I'll be fine here. I like it. It feels good being with the big kids." He smiled. But in the back of his mind, he was thinking just one thing—*Reed*. How was he going to stay out of Reed's way for eight whole weeks?

CHAPTER 5
UNEXPECTED OUTCOMES

"What are you doing, fairy darling?" asked Pixie as she peered over Jessie's shoulder. Jessie looked up and noticed the dark eyeliner and mascara that ringed Pixie's eyes. She looked like a messy raccoon. Jessie could imagine Pixie standing in front of the Big Dipper, eating frozen yogurt with the high school kids, who played music too loudly and flipped their skateboards over the curb.

Yet here she was, teacher of the class. It was a bit of a mystery.

"It's a blueprint," said Jessie. "For a bridge. A cantilever bridge. Which is very difficult to build because it relies on exact measurements of weight and counterweight. Too much this way or too little that way and—KABOOM." Jessie bent her head down over the drawing again. "So you see, I'm very busy."

She had taped large pieces of easel paper together to give her plenty of room, and the easel paper had grid lines on it, which was great for Jessie, because that helped her draw everything to scale. This was going to be a relatively small model of a cantilever bridge, just two feet long. A first attempt.

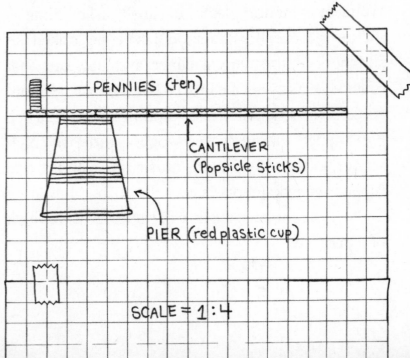

PENNIES (ten)

CANTILEVER
(Popsicle sticks)

PIER (red plastic cup)

SCALE = 1 : 4

She was using a scale of 1:4. If the drawing showed a piece of wood that was one inch long, then she knew she had to make the real piece of wood four inches long. Jessie liked scale drawings. They represented things that were *real*. Precise.

"Oh, sweetie pie," said Pixie, smiling and putting a hand on Jessie's shoulder. Jessie quickly slumped her shoulder so that Pixie's hand slipped off. "Your drawing is *so good*, but right now we have to get back to our fairy houses. It's already Wednesday. We all need to be finished by Friday, so we can set up our first fairy village on the playground. Won't that be fun?"

Jessie didn't respond. She had to calculate the length of the cantilever, the height of the support, and the heaviness of the counterweight. Jessie was using *The Great Big Book of Bridges* as her guide. It told her everything she needed to know. This was one of the reasons why Jessie liked books so much. More than people, really.

"I already finished mine," said Jessie, pointing

with her pencil at a fairy house, sitting on a table in the far corner of the room.

"But, Jessie, pumpkin! You couldn't have finished your house. We just started working on them yesterday . . . " Pixie's voice trailed off as she looked at Jessie's house across the room. She approached it slowly, as if she thought it might be a mirage.

"How did you make this?" Pixie's voice wasn't so twinkly and shimmery now. She sounded like a regular teenager.

Jessie kept her eyes on her drawing. "I made up blueprints yesterday after class, then I stayed up late building it at home." Jessie was like that. Once she got an idea, she had to keep at it until she was done. That's why Evan called her Obsessy Jessie. Not the nicest of nicknames, but not the worst! And she knew it was true. It's just the way she was.

"But . . . but . . . " Pixie bent low to get a good look at Jessie's fairy house.

The house stood about two feet tall. ("Two feet, three and a half inches," Jessie said, correcting her. "I can show you the blueprints.") It was surrounded by soft green moss. ("That's *not* for decoration," said Jessie. "It serves a purpose. It soaks up water from the ground to keep the floor dry. Moss is three times more absorbent than the average sponge.")

The house was a cylinder, covered neatly in latticework. ("That part fell off our porch," said Jessie. "It's good to recycle things.")

The roof was a perfect cone almost as tall as the house itself, sitting like a proud hat on top of the dwelling. The shingles on the roof were made from pine cones, carefully deconstructed, then put back together in this new shape.

"Wow. You used the petals of a pine cone," said Pixie. "How awesome!"

"They're not called 'petals,'" said Jessie patiently. "They're called 'scales.' And I used twenty-two and a half pine cones for the roof. It took a long time. That was the hardest part."

Pixie walked around the fairy house one more time. "I couldn't have made this if I'd spent the whole summer working on it."

"That?" asked Jessie. "That's nothing. It doesn't

even have a door or real windows or wiring for electricity. There's nothing inside. It's just . . . pretend! Fake! Things should be real. Not just make-believe."

Pixie turned to her and smiled. "I *like* make-believe," she said. "Sometimes, I like it better than what's real." She wandered back over to Jessie's table, where Jessie was measuring the distance between two squares on her grid paper. She had all her tools from home spread out in front of her: three sharp pencils and a sharpener, a big gummy eraser, a compass, a protractor, a ruler, tape, and a

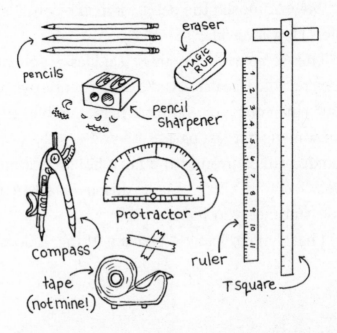

pencils

eraser

pencil
sharpener

compass

protractor

tape →
(not mine!)

ruler

T square

T square. "I borrowed your tape without asking," mumbled Jessie. "I forgot mine at home. I'm sorry."

"That's okay," said Pixie, looking closely at Jessie and smiling. Then she returned to her teacher's desk on the other side of the room to sort twigs into different piles.

From the other table, Jessie heard Becky say to Andrea and Lorelei, "She is such a mutant."

David flicked a folded triangle of paper at Becky. "It's the best house in the whole class—better than yours, better than mine." David's house was tilting seriously to one side. It looked like a birthday cake with baking powder in just one half.

"Oh, give me a break!" said Becky, keeping a close eye on Pixie across the room. "Jessie's a complete alien from another planet, and everyone knows it."

All the other kids were looking at Jessie, even Katrina, who seemed confused and a little afraid. Jessie felt her face go hot, and she knew her neck was getting those funny red splotches that *did* make her look like an alien from another planet. She kept asking herself, *Why does she hate me so much? What did I do?*

"Becky!" sang Pixie in her zither voice. "Fairies don't use words like 'alien from another planet.' But they do have kind words like *ovanlig*, which means 'spectacularly original.' And I would say Jessie's house is entirely *ovanlig*."

"Fairies aren't real," said Jessie resolutely. "And neither is the word *ovanlig*!" She didn't think it was right for a teacher to say there was a fairy language when it wasn't true—although it made her *zing* inside to hear Pixie say that her house was *spectacular*. Jessie loved it when she got credit for her work. The best kind of attention was applause. That's one of the reasons she was entering the bridge-building contest. The winners would be announced in an auditorium filled with people. She imagined everyone clapping when she went on stage to get her prize.

"I believe in fairies," Katrina said, smiling from across the table.

Jessie opened her mouth, but Pixie said, "So do I, Katrina! And anyone who doesn't can have fun by pretending."

Katrina continued to smile and waved a piece of birch bark like a flag in a Fourth of July parade.

Jessie practiced biting her tongue. *There are no such things as fairies,* she told herself. *And they wouldn't live in houses covered in glitter, because hiding would be a fairy's best defense.* If fairies existed. Which they definitely didn't.

After lunch, David crossed the room to look at Jessie's drawing of her cantilever bridge.

"Isn't that going to tip and fall into the water?" he asked.

"It might. Cantilever bridges are tricky. That's why I'm going to test it before I build the real thing." She reached down into her backpack and retrieved her hot-glue gun, along with a large bag of Popsicle sticks and a stack of red plastic cups that she and Evan used for lemonade stands. "Here," she said to David, "you can hold the bag of pennies."

Using the quick-drying glue, Jessie attached a long "arm" made from Popsicle sticks to the bottom of a red cup, with a shorter arm sticking out in the opposite direction. The whole thing immediately tipped over.

"See," said David, but not in a mean way. "Why didn't you make both sides even? The long part is always going to fall over. Is it a mistake?"

Jessie said, "First of all: The greatest engineers make mistakes every day. It's how they build amazing things that have never been built before. And they're not called mistakes; they're called 'unexpected outcomes.' Engineers learn from unexpected outcomes. Second: My model is *not* a mistake. It's exactly the way I want it to be."

She placed a second red plastic cup under the long end, so that the bridge rested evenly. Katrina wandered over to see what was going on. She had a streak of red marker across her cheek.

"Okay," said Jessie. "Let's start with ten pennies. Put them on the short end, right there."

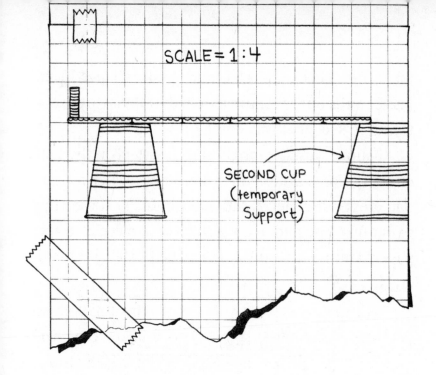

SCALE = 1 : 4

SECOND CUP
(temporary
Support)

David placed ten pennies on the short end of the bridge. Jessie slowly pulled the second plastic cup away from the long end. The bridge collapsed! The pennies made a loud clattering sound as they hit the hard, polished stone of the art table and began to roll. David and Katrina shouted "Oh!" and did their best to catch the coins before they fell to the floor. The commotion brought Ava over to Jessie's table, but Becky, Lorelei, and Andrea stayed put. Jessie noticed that Andrea looked in their direction, trying to see what was going on.

"Failure number one!" said Jessie proudly. Her cheeks were slightly pink and the tip of her tongue had crept out of her mouth and settled in the corner of her lips. She had made a chart on a piece of graph paper, and next to the box marked "10" she made an X.

ATTEMPT NUMBER	NUMBER OF PENNIES	FAIL X SUCCESS ✓
1	10	X
2	20	
3	30	
4	40	
5	50	
6	60	

"Now let's try twenty." She put the second red cup back in its place as a temporary support.

David piled twenty pennies on the short end of the deck. Jessie removed the red cup. The bridge crashed to the table, and the pennies scattered. The kids hurried to gather the pennies so they could try again.

Pixie came to the table with her pencil stuck in her hair and said that these were the kinds of games that real fairies play.

By the time they were up to forty pennies, everyone in the fairy house class had gathered around the table except for Becky. She continued to play with the necklace around her neck, sliding the rose quartz pendant back and forth on its chain. Occasionally she shouted out a discouraging comment like "What a waste of time!" or "You can't make a bridge out of Popsicle sticks!"

Finally, when David had piled *sixty* pennies on the short arm, the bridge held! It was beautiful—stretching into the distance as if it could reach eternity. All the fairies clapped their hands and Pixie did a pirouette, waving her wand over all of their heads.

"How does it do that?" asked Katrina. "Why doesn't it fall over?"

Jessie explained: "This is the basic principle of a cantilever bridge. The plastic cup is the *support,* the pennies are the *counterweight,* and the Popsicle sticks make the *cantilever.* Once the force of the counterweight equals the force of the cantilever, they're in balance on the support. But obviously, to finish the bridge you need a cantilever on the other side. Like this." She made a quick drawing that showed two cantilevers together to form a complete bridge.

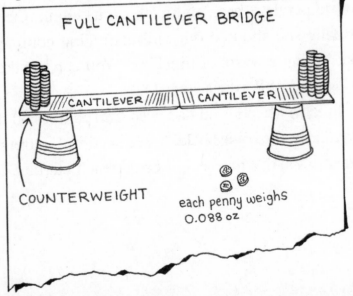

FULL CANTILEVER BRIDGE

CANTILEVER / CANTILEVER

COUNTERWEIGHT

each penny weighs
0.088 oz

"But we're not done yet," said Jessie. She reached over and took one penny away.

The bridge stayed.

Everyone watched, silently.

She reached over and took another penny away.

The bridge stayed.

"Oh, Jessie!" whispered Katrina. "Don't do it!"

"We have to," whispered Jessie back. "This is what it means to do an experiment. We have to find the exact counterweight needed to keep the bridge from falling down."

She took away another penny.

And another.

When she took the fifth penny away, the whole bridge collapsed. The classroom erupted with groans, and Pixie covered her eyes. "I can't stand it!" she squealed.

But Jessie was busy filling in her chart. "That was fifty-five pennies. Each penny weighs 0.088 ounces, which means the correct counterweight for this bridge is 4.84 ounces." She reached down into her backpack and retrieved a small toy car.

"I already weighed this at home, so I know it weighs 2.3 ounces, which is the same as twenty-seven pennies. So if we add twenty-seven and fifty-five, that means we need eighty-two pennies as a counterweight."

David was already counting, and soon he had the right amount to place on the short end of the bridge. Then Jessie lined up the small car on top of the plastic cup just in front of the pile of pennies.

"Wait!" shouted Katrina. "Let me get my troll!" She ran to the other table and came back with a hideous plastic monster that looked exactly like the kind of thing that would live under a bridge. Half its magenta hair was missing, and Katrina had blacked out all of its teeth. She positioned the troll on the table where the long arm of the bridge ended.

"Why do you have a troll?" asked Jessie.

"I have two," said Katrina. "The other one has a sparkly diamond necklace! They're planning to attack my fairy house. I'm working on a magic spell to keep my special fairy safe."

Jessie opened her mouth. Absolutely everything Katrina had said was completely and totally and absolutely wrong. There were no attacking trolls. There were no magic spells. And there definitely were *no fairies*.

"Let it go, Jessie," said David, which Jessie realized was exactly the kind of thing Evan would have said if he were there. "Just do the thing with the car. And besides, the troll adds a really cool effect." He pointed.

He was right. The troll stood underneath the long end of the bridge, its thick arms reaching up to devour the car if it fell off the bridge.

"Okay," said Jessie. "Here goes." She inched the car forward, bit by bit, Popsicle stick by Popsicle stick. When the car was almost halfway down the length of the bridge, everybody in the room got really quiet, as if they were afraid to breathe. Even Jessie held her breath for the last few inches.

When she gave the final push so that the car was perched on the very end of the bridge with the troll staring up at it, its evil grasping hands reaching to grab it, the bridge held steady. Everybody in the class shouted and jumped in the air and gave each other high fives and low fives and medium fives. Jessie just sat back on her stool and stared at what she'd made. She had done it. She had built one half of a cantilever bridge. And it could carry a real load, just like a real bridge in the real world. And if she built another one and put the two in a line, she would have made a bridge that could cross over water or a highway without any supports in the middle. That's what was so cool about cantilevers. They seemed to float.

Katrina wriggled up beside her and asked, "How does it do that? Is it magic?"

"No," said Jessie. "It's science."

David noticed it first. A bright color out of the corner of his eye. An unexpected glint as the afternoon sunlight fell across the room. Something out of place. Something wrong.

"Jessie! Your house!" he said.

Everyone looked across the room.

Jessie's fairy house—the one with the moss and the latticework and the perfectly pointed roof made out of pine-cone scales—was covered in a gluey, gloppy mountain of purple glitter.

CHAPTER 6
FRIDAY #1

Jessie! Evan suddenly thought of his sister and looked up from the basketball he'd been dribbling by himself.

It was Friday, the last day of the first week of summer school. He'd never wished for a weekend so badly in all his life. If he could just stay out of Reed's way. If he could just make it to the end of the day, he'd have two whole days away from him.

And then it would start again. Seven more weeks. It felt like summer was going to last forever.

Evan looked across the middle school field to where the wetlands and stream divided this school from Hillside. It was a long way, but he could see Jessie sitting at a picnic table. He could tell it was her because of her lemon-yellow T-shirt. It was one of her favorites. She was sitting next to someone. Who was it? Evan shaded his eyes from the afternoon sun and looked again. Was it . . . David Kirkorian?

No!

David K. had been in Evan and Jessie's class last year, and he was a *strange kid*. People said he had all kinds of weird collections. Human brains in jars. And rats' teeth. Evan didn't believe those rumors, but David K. was definitely an oddball.

And then a thought entered Evan's head and bounced around like the basketball in his hands. *Kind of like me.* For the first time in his life, Evan felt like the one who didn't belong. It was strange, he thought, that you could be exactly the same person in two different places. In one place, you were the king, but in the other place, *you* were the one who didn't fit in. The one who was left out.

He started bouncing the ball again, away from the other kids. He had brought his own ball from home, but nobody else wanted to play. Basketball, it turned out, was not Reed's game.

Evan glanced around the blacktop and fields. Stevie was sitting at one of the picnic tables, hunched over and secretive. Reed and his gang were hanging off the top bars of the soccer nets, which was against the rules. At least it was in elementary school. Evan didn't really know the rules of middle school. Another way he didn't fit in.

Evan dribbled his ball to the edge of the blacktop and then walked across the field toward the stream. When he reached it, he called out, "Hey, Jessie!" The stream was four feet across and only six inches deep, but the water was murky and it was common knowledge among the kids that there were water snakes under the surface. The stream was a boundary no one would cross. "Jessie!"

Jessie looked up and immediately trotted over. She stood on her side of the stream and Evan stood on his. Four feet had never felt so far.

"What?" asked Jessie.

Evan glanced over his shoulder. He didn't want any of the older kids seeing him talking to his little sister. "What are you doing?" he asked.

"Planning the next model," said Jessie. "A cable-stayed bridge. Very complicated." She frowned. "So, what do you want?" She glanced over her shoulder too, and suddenly Evan felt like she wanted to get back to what she'd been doing with David K.

Evan didn't know what to say. Why *had* he crossed the field to see her?

"You look strange," said Jessie. "Why aren't you playing with your friends?" She pointed at the crowd of boys hanging on the soccer nets. "They're not supposed to do that at recess."

"It's not called recess here!" snapped Evan.

Jessie looked surprised. Evan didn't usually snap like that. He was usually the one in the good mood.

"I'm sorry," said Evan, nudging a small rock into the water with his foot. "I just— Everything is really weird on this side."

"It's too bad you can't come over to this side,"

said Jessie. "We're having fun building bridges. In fact, David K. says I've taken over the class."

Jessie looked pretty pleased about this, and Evan knew that his little sister was happiest when she was in charge. Or at least *thought* she was.

"So it *is* David K. you're sitting with?" asked Evan, looking at the lone figure at the table waiting for Jessie to return.

"Wait! Listen!" Jessie said suddenly. She froze still and Evan did the same, both scanning the tall grasses around them. "There!" whispered Jessie. She pointed. When Evan looked, he could see a goose sitting on a nest about thirty feet away from them. She was looking straight at them, but she didn't seem alarmed.

"Wow," said Evan. "Right here. In the middle of *this*."

By "this" he meant "summer school," which he thought was way too miserable a place for something as amazing as new life coming into the world.

How was it possible that baby geese could peck

their way through a smooth, hard shell and learn to swim in this little stream, but only a few hundred yards away Reed had stuck Stevie's feet in the boys' bathroom toilet? The world was a strange place, and it sure seemed like it was going to get even stranger over the next seven weeks.

"That's why we're not supposed to be here," said Jessie, who liked to follow rules. "There are five pairs of nesting geese, and we're supposed to leave them alone. Besides, I don't like geese."

"I know, I know," said Evan. "They poop." But Evan liked looking at the goose, sitting quietly on her mound of dried grass and leaves, nestled securely in the wetlands. She seemed to know exactly what she was doing, and Evan felt a sense of comfort—and envy—in that.

"So, what's going on with the mean girls?" asked Evan. Jessie had told Evan about Becky on Monday, as soon as he got home from summer school. He had told her to stay as far away from Becky as possible.

"Becky dumped a ton of purple glitter on my fairy house! But no one saw her do it, so my teacher won't kick her out of the class. Which I think would be the fair thing to do. She's mean. You were right about that, and David said the same thing about her."

"I'm sorry, Jess," said Evan. "I hate it when kids are mean."

"You know what I discovered?" Her eyes widened, the way they did when she learned a new fact about mushroom spores or outer space or volcanoes. *I don't care!* Really! David said this, and he's right: 'Who cares what she thinks?' Can she build a cantilever bridge out of Popsicle sticks and plastic cups? Does she know how tension and compression keep a bridge from falling down? Is she going to win the bridge-building contest in two weeks? I don't think so! She's just mean. And that's *nothing.*"

Evan wished he could feel that way about Reed.

"I've got to get back. See ya!" Jessie was already hurrying to the picnic table where David was waiting.

Evan stared at his little sister. How had she learned so much at one week of Summer Fun Exploration Camp when he hadn't learned anything at all at summer school? Except to stay out of the boys' bathroom when Reed was around.

When Evan got back to the other kids, they were filing into the building. Their break was over too. Evan scanned the crowd but didn't see Stevie. He asked a girl whose name he didn't know if she knew where he was.

The girl answered in a whisper. "He got shoved on the stairs," she said, pointing to the concrete steps that led from the upper field to the walkway. "They took him to the nurse." She dropped her voice even lower. "There was blood."

Evan didn't need to ask who had pushed Stevie, just as the girl hadn't needed to say it out loud. He wondered what would have happened if he'd been there when the teasing had started. Would he have stepped up to protect Stevie? Would he have watched, silently, frozen, with all the others? Or would he have turned his back and gone on shooting free throws, trying to pretend that the whole thing wasn't happening at all?

He dribbled the ball once or twice, staring toward the picnic table where Stevie had been sitting alone during the break. Lost in thought, he didn't have time to react when the ball was snatched out of his hands.

"Hey!" said Evan.

"Let's see how far this thing can fly," said Reed. He tossed the ball in the air and then drop-kicked it as hard as he could. It sailed over the fence and into the thick scrub that bordered the school on that side.

The scrub was a tangled mess full of poison ivy and biting mosquitoes. It would be impossible for Evan to find his ball in there. If something landed in the scrub, it never came out.

"You can't do that!" shouted Evan, still shocked that his ball had been stolen from him.

"Except that I just did," said Reed, walking toward the door, where his friends were waiting for him, laughing.

Evan stared at where the ball had fallen from sight. He had done extra house chores for two months to save up to buy that ball. And now it was gone. Forever.

As he stared toward the scrub, he saw something on the picnic table. Evan jogged over to the table to see what it was.

Three medieval knights in full armor, each one the size of his thumb and made out of metal, stood ready to do battle. One had a long sword raised, prepared to fight. Another had a club lifted over his head, ready to smash down on his enemy. The third seemed to be running at full speed. In his right hand was a short sword, in his left a shield protecting his flank, as if he feared an attack from behind. But whether the soldier was running to the battle or away from it, Evan couldn't tell.

Evan thought of Stevie sitting in the nurse's office, probably with a bloody knee or shin, or maybe something worse. He scooped up the three toy soldiers, put them in the side pocket of his cargo shorts, and headed into class.

As everyone was settling in, the girl who had answered Evan's question about Stevie asked Evan, "What were you doing on the edge of the field?"

Evan didn't want to admit that he was talking to his little sister, so he said, "There are some geese over there and I just wanted to see if I could find a nest. I found one, and I think it has eggs in it." It felt good to share this small miracle with someone who had been worried about Stevie.

"Geese?" asked a loud voice behind them. "You mean like sitting on actual eggs?"

Reed.

Suddenly, Evan wished he'd kept his mouth shut.

"No," said Evan. "I looked, but I didn't find any. The geese are dangerous, you know. They attack if you get close to their nest." He felt like he was spinning the pedals on his bike backwards, as if he could go in reverse, undoing what he had just done.

And that's when Evan got his new nickname.

"Nice try, Goose Boy," said Reed, smiling wickedly.

"Come on," said Mrs. Warner. "Settle! It shouldn't take this long to transition. Back into your seats. Enough talking. We're here to learn."

But Evan couldn't settle. His heart was beating hard against his ribs, and he felt as though he had metal bands around his chest. The bands kept tightening as he imagined the goose sitting quietly on her nest and Reed approaching through the tall grass.

Tightening, tightening, tightening.

On the way home that afternoon, Evan was walking up West Street, purposely lagging behind the other kids. By the end of the school day, Reed and all his friends were calling him Goose Boy. They were ahead of him now, and he didn't want to accidentally catch up and give them the chance to tease him more.

He shouldn't have worried, though, because Stevie was even further up the sidewalk. Evan noticed the extra-large Band-Aid covering one of Stevie's elbows, probably from his "fall" down the stairs.

"Albert! Hey, Albert!" Reed and his friends were picking up pine cones and lobbing them at Stevie.

Except it wasn't really lobbing. They were throwing pretty hard. Stevie kept ducking and walking as fast as he could. But the other boys were getting closer.

Reed ran out of pine cones, and Evan saw him reach down and pick up a rock. It was pretty small, but when he threw it at Stevie, he threw it hard, the way he'd been throwing the pine cones. It missed, but then the other boys picked up rocks too, and some of them had better aim than Reed. Some of them were hitting Stevie in his arms and legs and his rear end and back.

Stevie was trying to act like nothing was happening. If you paid attention, though, the way Evan was, you could see him flinch every time a rock hit him. And he kept walking as fast as he could up the hill. West Street was a busy road with a lot of traffic. Plenty of drivers were going by, but not one driver stopped to yell at Reed and his friends. Not one grownup told them to leave that kid alone and *act decent.*

Evan saw it all, though. He knew exactly what was going on, and he knew exactly what he should do. But instead, his body walked more and more slowly. He told himself it wasn't his fight. He had enough to worry about on his own.

And then the boys started running toward Stevie, getting closer so that more and more of their shots hit the mark. And they were starting to wedge themselves between Stevie and the high wall that ran along that part of the sidewalk, so that Stevie was slowly inching toward the street in an effort to avoid the worst blows. He was getting closer and closer to the busy road, and the boys were herding him there, laughing and shouting so that anyone driving by might think it was just a game that boys play.

Evan knew he should try to stop Reed and those boys. He knew he should call for help, flag down one of the passing cars and tell a grownup what was really going on. At the very least, he should sprint up the hill and put himself between Stevie and those boys, yank Stevie back from the edge of the sidewalk where he was now in danger of falling into the street, with the oncoming traffic and no one doing anything to help. He should *do something*.

But he didn't. He didn't.

He couldn't.

And then a chipmunk ran right in front of the boys, surprising them and making them stop as they tried to figure out where it had gone. Stevie hurried ahead, crossed High Street against the light, and ran as if his life depended on it.

When Evan got home, his mother said, "Are you all right? You look sick."

He wanted to tell her what had happened. He wanted to tell her about the knot in his stomach. The knowledge that he couldn't do anything to help Stevie. The knowledge, just as certain, that he could have.

But he couldn't tell her, because then she would know. She thought he was the kind of kid who stands up for anyone who needs standing up for.

The kind of kid that other kids turn to. *A natural-born leader.*

That's what she thought. But it turned out that it wasn't true. And if he told her the story of what had happened that afternoon, if he told her all of it—about being called Goose Boy and the pebbles flying through the air and Stevie shoved down the concrete steps—she would know that he wasn't who she thought he was. And he would have to know it about himself.

So he said nothing.

CHAPTER 7
SNEAKY PEOPLE

"I definitely want a drawbridge for my next house," said David as they walked into the art room for the start of the second week of Summer Fun Exploration Camp. He had already changed his mind three times in the hallway. First he had wanted a suspension bridge. Then definitely a beam. Then probably a cantilever. At one point, he'd wanted all three.

"And *I* want the kind with the triangles all along the side," said Katrina, who was already spinning on her stool. "Because they're pretty, and make the bridge super strong. To fight the trolls!" She jumped off her stool and did a kick to the side with one leg and then a kick to the other side with the other leg, all while wearing a skirt made out of floaty white netting covered in sparkling sequins. Jessie had to admit: Katrina would make one fierce fairy.

"A truss bridge," said Jessie. "Here." She handed Katrina a piece of paper. "I drew a picture for you over the weekend."

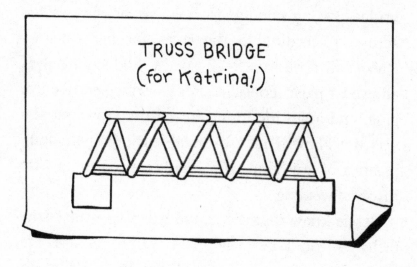

TRUSS BRIDGE
(for Katrina!)

Jessie had had a busy weekend. She had gotten her second fairy house out of the way so that she could concentrate on her bridge this week at camp. Pixie didn't seem to mind. As long as everyone finished three houses by the end of the session, she was satisfied.

The deadline for the bridge contest was in two weeks—Saturday to be exact. Now that Jessie had finished her blueprints, she was ready to start building. Her entry would be a six-foot-long suspension bridge, strong enough to hold *her* as she walked across. According to the rules for her category ("Most Innovative, 9–12 Years Old"), she was allowed to use Popsicle sticks, string, cardboard, glue, and anything found in nature. However, she was not allowed to use metal (including tin foil), plastics of any kind, wire, nails, or anything that involved welding.

Jessie knew that the key to winning—the "wow factor"—would be when she walked across the bridge in front of the judges. As far as she knew, no

one in the history of the contest had ever tested their entry by using themselves as the load. It's what made her bridge "most innovative." Even *she* wasn't sure it was possible. But she knew if she couldn't build a bridge strong enough to walk over, she wouldn't win. And Jessie couldn't stand the thought of someone else getting all the applause that came with being the winner.

This morning, Jessie had stuffed her backpack full of Popsicle sticks. The other campers drifted in, and Becky managed to kick Jessie's stool on the way to her own seat. The sudden jolt caused Jessie to scratch her pencil across her drawing.

Pixie floated in from the hallway. "Good morning, sleepy fairies. Happy Monday to you all. Did everyone sleep well in their nutshells last night?"

Oh, brother, thought Jessie.

"I did! I did!" said Katrina, waving her hands, which were covered in glue. She jumped off her stool. "See my fairy skirt! See how it twirls!" Then she did a series of spins and kicks that looked surprisingly vicious, despite the light-as-air skirt.

Pixie scooted Katrina back to her stool and then said, "Today we're going to . . . We're going to . . ." Her voice trailed off, and there were tears in her eyes. Jessie knew what tears meant: *sad.* Except once in a while, they meant *happy.* It was very confusing.

"Do you need a glass of water?" asked Jessie.

"I think maybe I do," said Pixie. She took a few noisy gulps from her water bottle. (*Very unfairylike!* thought Jessie.) "Come along, little fairies," she said. "Into our wonderland we go! It's time to draw pictures for our new and wonderful houses. I've brought in something very special for you this week." She opened a large trash bag that she pulled from behind her desk and scooped out a handful of acorns to show them. "I spent the whole weekend collecting them."

She demonstrated how to separate the cap from the nut: the cap could be a little fairy plate and the nut could be a fairy cup. Then the class got to work drawing pictures of fairy houses with acorns—acorn chandeliers, acorn tables, acorn staircases.

David edged closer to Jessie's seat.

"I don't want to make another house," whispered David. "Can I help you with your bridge instead?"

But before Jessie could answer, Becky swooped in and whispered, "Nice going, freak. You made Pixie cry!"

Jessie looked around the room. Why would asking someone if they wanted a glass of water make them cry? And besides! Pixie was crying before Jessie said anything!

But Jessie could see that Pixie *was* hiding behind the open door to one of the paint closets.

"Do you think she's crying?" Jessie asked David.

"It's hard to tell. Maybe she's just checking her phone. Older kids do that a lot."

"Kids?" asked Jessie. "She's the teacher."

"Well, she's only in college. She's the same age as my oldest brother. They went to high school together. Last year!"

Jessie frowned. She did not think it was right for a college student to be teaching a class. And she did not think it was right for a teacher to pretend that fairies were real. And she *really* did not think it was right for a teacher—any teacher—to hide behind the open door of a paint closet.

"This is ridiculous," said Jessie. If there was one thing Jessie didn't like, it was people not doing what they were supposed to do. Scott Spencer cutting in line. The horrible substitute teacher Mrs. Feeney not even trying to teach them about poetry when Mrs. Overton was absent. Jessie's father, leaving them once, and then coming back just so he could leave them again, without even saying goodbye to her. And—as far as Jessie was concerned—crying camp fairy teachers were not doing *anything* right. Jessie would have to do something about it.

She walked across the room and opened the paint closet door all the way. "Are you crying?"

Pixie turned around, surprised. Her eyes were red and wet, and there was a little round globule of snot hanging from one of her nostrils. (*Definitely not fairylike!* thought Jessie.) "I'm just not . . ." Pixie's voice wavered. "I'm not having a very good day."

Jessie thought about this piece of information. It did not make sense. It was only nine o'clock in the morning. It was too early to decide if today was a good day or a bad day.

"Why?" she asked.

"Jessie!" said Pixie, exasperated. She smooshed

the palm of one hand against her face, trying to wipe away tears without looking like she was. A black smear of makeup streaked across her cheek. "It's *complicated*. It's not something I can just *explain*."

Jessie stopped to think about that, too. "Why not?" she asked. She thought about the invisible forces—*tension* and *compression*—that work to keep a bridge from falling apart. *That* was complicated. If Jessie could explain that idea to Katrina (which she had), then Pixie could definitely explain why she was having a bad day.

Pixie twisted her index finger into the edge of her T-shirt, twining it tighter and tighter.

"It's just that . . . the camp director . . . Mrs. Richter . . . the one who runs the whole program . . . she said . . . that . . . that . . . there was a *complaint* filed against me . . . by one of the *parents*. And that if it happens again . . . I would be . . . *replaced*."

"Does that mean 'fired'?" asked Jessie.

"It sounds even worse when you say it like that,"

said Pixie, her eyes filling again with tears. She untwisted her index finger and used the hem of her T-shirt to wipe her nose. "I wasn't even supposed to teach this class. My mom was. She planned the whole thing. She used to be a teacher. But then she had to have surgery."

"She had to have surgery when she was a teacher?" asked Jessie.

"No! Just three weeks ago. She's totally fine, but she needs to stay in bed for *six* weeks, and I thought I could help. You know. Show her that I'm not such a . . . mess-up. I just wanted to prove that I could help. Like a grownup."

"You're not a grownup," Jessie pointed out. "Anyone can see that. Maybe you'd look more like a grownup if you weren't wearing fairy wings."

"We thought the class would get canceled!" said Pixie. "Not enough kids signed up. But then, at the very last minute, one more kid signed up, just enough, and it was too late to tell Mrs. Richter that my mom couldn't do it, so I said *I'd* do it."

David K.! thought Jessie. If he hadn't signed up for the class, Jessie could have spent three whole weeks working on her entry for the bridge-building contest and Pixie could have stayed home with her mom. Three weeks! She could have built two suspension bridges in that time!

"I've tried," said Pixie. "I really have."

"Tried what?" asked Jessie.

"To be a good fairy! And a good teacher! But someone complained! And it's another mess-up. Which is pretty much what I always do!"

Pixie started to cry again. Katrina came over and slipped one of her gluey hands into Pixie's and gave it a squeeze.

"Who complained?" asked Jessie.

"It was anonymous," said Pixie through her tears.

"I don't like sneaky people," Jessie said. "Why didn't that person just tell you to your face? That's the way we do it at our house. I tell my mom what's bugging me all the time." Jessie glared. "I don't like sneaky people." She was staring right at Becky when she said it.

"It doesn't matter who," said Pixie. She wiped her face again and sighed. Then she twirled Katrina once so that Katrina's fairy skirt flared out and told her to go back to her seat. "It just matters that someone said the class was boring and that doing the same thing for three weeks was no fun. That's why I spent the weekend collecting acorns. I thought it would make a difference. But I don't think it's enough."

"It's not," said Jessie flatly. "Acorns aren't very interesting. You know what's interesting? Bridges. Bridges are *fascinating*."

CHAPTER 8
OUT OF THE SCRUB
AND ONTO THE ROOF

"Hey, Goose Boy!" said a voice. "There's poison ivy in there."

Evan looked up from the scrub to see Reed on the other side of the fence, staring back at him. *Great*, he thought. *Of all people.*

"Leaves of three, leave them be," said Reed, idly reciting the well-known advice about poison ivy. It was hot, and Reed sounded bored as he whacked the fence with a branch he had torn off a tree.

Evan expected him to keep walking, but Reed

looked like he had nowhere to go. Evan had been searching for his basketball for almost an hour, and he was hot and scratched up from the thorny bushes that tangled themselves throughout the scrub. In frustration, he said, "You could help me look."

"I am helping. I'm *looking*," said Reed, still whacking at the fence and not looking for the ball at all. "But there ain't no way you're goin' to get me into the scrub. That's just dumb."

Evan gritted his teeth. He wanted his basketball back, even if it meant his whole body getting covered in itchy, oozing poison ivy sores. It was *his* ball, and he wasn't going to lose it because of a kid like Reed.

"Hey, there it is," said Reed, pointing with his stick to a spot where some thick bushes grew.

Evan didn't see it, but Reed directed him, deeper and deeper into the scrub. At one point, Evan thought he'd found it, but it was just a faded orange Frisbee. He tossed the plastic disk over the fence and kept looking where Reed pointed.

"There!"

Suddenly Evan saw it and grabbed the ball. He fought his way out of the scrub and scrambled over the fence.

Reed was twirling the orange Frisbee on his finger like a spinning plate. "You want to throw some?" he asked Evan.

"No," said Evan. "I gotta go home." He hated this kid. Hated everything about him, from the way he treated Stevie to the way he treated his own friends.

"C'mon! Don't be a loser." Reed started to run across the field and shouted, "Go long!" Then with one fluid movement that ended in a wicked flick of his wrist, he sent the Frisbee soaring through the air.

Deep in Evan's DNA, there was coding that told him to catch things when they were thrown and to throw things that he'd caught. It was an instinct from his youngest days and part of what made him a great athlete. His mother once told Evan he was part Labrador retriever.

Evan dropped his basketball and ran to catch the flying disk. He couldn't stop himself.

"Over-the-shoulder catch! Awesome!" crowed Reed. "Throw it back."

And Evan did.

Reed was really good at Frisbee. Better than Evan. They played for about ten minutes, and then Reed said, "Hey, look," and pointed to the marshy area between the two schools. "I bet I can hit that goose." Reed started to measure the distance with his eyes and then took a few practice steps in the direction of the goose. "It's like a sitting duck! Get it?" He laughed at his own joke.

"Don't!" said Evan. He took off toward the goose, hoping to startle her into the water.

Reed winged the Frisbee sidearm, low and hard. Evan couldn't reach the goose in time, but he threw himself forward, stretching his full body length, and was able to block the Frisbee in midflight. He banged his shoulder pretty hard on the grass when he landed, but the goose, sitting on her nest, was safe.

"Aw, c'mon," shouted Reed, throwing his arms up in disgust. "I could have hit that thing!"

"Well, you didn't," said Evan, holding on to the

Frisbee while he retrieved his basketball.

"Give me the Frisbee," said Reed.

"No," said Evan.

"C'mon," said Reed.

"Not unless you promise to leave the goose alone," said Evan, walking toward the school.

"You really are Goose Boy," said Reed, shaking his head with pity. "C'mon. Give me the Frisbee."

"No."

Reed started walking toward him, and without thinking, Evan threw the Frisbee with all his might. He was aiming for the high branches of the trees on the other side of the school, but his aim was off and the Frisbee landed on the flat roof of the school.

Both boys stared at the spot where the Frisbee had disappeared. Reed looked really angry. Evan wondered if he was about to get into a fistfight—his first ever. He'd broken up a few in his life, mostly playground squabbles between kids who were smaller than him. But he'd never taken a real swing at anyone.

"*You* are going up there with me to get that Frisbee," said Reed.

"We can't go on the roof," said Evan.

"Didn't you hear me? I want that Frisbee, and you're coming with me to get it."

There was something truly dangerous about Reed—what kind of person throws something at a mother goose sitting on a nest full of eggs? Maybe the safest thing for the goose was for Evan to go up on the roof to keep Reed from exploding.

Reed knew exactly how to get on the roof; it was clear he'd done this before. Behind the dumpsters was a metal fire escape ladder that hung six feet above the blacktop. Evan put down his basketball, and Reed gave him a one-up so that Evan could reach the lowest rung. Then Reed jumped—his vertical jump was surprisingly good—and shimmied up himself.

The roof was littered with balls, shoes, sticks, and other Frisbees. Reed picked up the faded orange one, ignoring all the rest, and said, "Now we're going to play up here. If you don't catch what I throw and the Frisbee lands on the blacktop, you lose."

"No," said Evan. "I'm not going to do that." Evan immediately understood that the game would encourage each boy to throw the Frisbee to a spot as close to the edge of the roof as possible, in the hope that the other boy wouldn't catch it in time. There was no fence to keep you from falling off the roof, not even a rise at the edge to let you know you were close to falling. This was a dangerous game, and Evan wanted no part of it.

"Do you know," asked Reed casually, tossing the Frisbee vertically a few feet and catching it, "that I can turn you into Albert anytime I want? I've been nice to you so far, but I don't have to be."

Evan heard the words his mother had said to Evan and Jessie over the years: *Don't let anyone tell you who you are or what you're capable of.* But here on the hot roof with Reed standing between him and the ladder, those words didn't offer him any way out. He looked at the edge of the roof and saw the shimmering blacktop, twelve feet below. "You can't make me," said Evan.

"Sure I can," said Reed with a low cackle. "Things are different in middle school. Haven't you figured that out yet?"

I'm not *a bad kid,* Evan thought. *I'm a natural-born leader.* But he was starting to understand how things worked in this new place. What caused him to be a leader in elementary school was exactly what made him an outcast in middle school. The rules were different here, and everyone else had a head start on learning them.

Reed backed up until his heels were resting on the edge of the roof. "Go long," he said as he wound up.

It was a gentle throw. The flat part of the roof wasn't much bigger than a basketball court. Still, the Frisbee was sailing for the far edge, and Evan would have to run as fast as he could to catch it. How was he going to stop, even if he made it there in time? The surface of the roof was covered in pebbles, which meant there was no traction. At a full run, you would skid six feet before coming to a stop.

Evan took off. He thought he could make the catch. The Frisbee was making a slow arc through the hot midday air. But even as he charged forward, Evan could tell that the point of intersection between the Frisbee and his hands was going to be a few feet past the edge of the roof.

He was going to fall. He should stop. He kept going.

And then a soft breeze blew across the asphalt heat of the roof and lifted the Frisbee higher. It was a back wind that slowed down the Frisbee and caused it to hover at its highest point. This gave Evan the three extra steps he needed. He jumped, caught the flying disk, and pulled it into his chest as he skidded to a stop about six inches from the edge.

Evan took three deep breaths, then wound up and threw the Frisbee as hard and high as he could so that it landed in a tree branch fifty feet off the ground.

"Hey!" said Reed. "You lose! You didn't keep the Frisbee on the roof."

"That wasn't the rule," said Evan, still panting. "You said if the Frisbee lands on the blacktop, you lose. Well, it's not on the blacktop, and it's never going to be."

Evan walked past Reed to the ladder and climbed down. He picked up his basketball and as he walked away, he heard Reed shout, "Bye, Albert!"

CHAPTER 9
THE BET

"Your shoelaces aren't tied," said Jessie as they put their lunches in their backpacks.

It was Evan's turn to make their lunches, and Jessie knew that meant her peanut butter and jelly sandwich would have too much peanut butter and not enough jelly. She sighed. She wished her mother had time to make the lunches, but her mom had a really tight deadline on a huge project, and she'd been working fourteen-hour days just to get the work done.

"They're untied on *both* shoes," added Jessie, astonished that Evan could be so careless.

"I know," said Evan. "I want them that way."

"Why?" asked Jessie. "You'll trip."

"I won't trip."

"But you could," said Jessie. "And your shoes might fall off. Look! They're practically falling off now! Every time you take a step. It's dangerous."

"This is how all the kids at school wear them," said Evan.

"*All* the kids at school?" asked Jessie, who liked statements of fact to be very precise. "I don't think *all* of them do. That would be very strange."

"Bye, Jess."

"You said you'd help me carry half of my bridge to school today." It was Friday, and Evan had been promising since Wednesday to help Jessie carry the three-foot section of her suspension bridge to school. She needed the long art table because there wasn't any table at home long enough for the finished bridge.

With the contest in just one week, Jessie was

worried about finishing her entry. Gluing thousands of Popsicle sticks took a long time, and she'd already had one section collapse because she'd built it in a hurry.

"Sorry, can't. I'm late," said Evan, already through the door. "Next week, I promise."

He was gone.

Slowly, Jessie put her lunch in her backpack. There was definitely something different about Evan. This whole week, he hadn't been acting like himself. He was combing his hair a different way, and disappearing after school most afternoons. Yesterday, when she'd suggested walking into town together to get ice cream cones, he'd said no, even though he was sitting on the couch playing a video game. *Who says no to ice cream?*

Jessie was only half a block from her house when David K. appeared, jogging to catch up with her. Every day! It was like he was waiting for her.

They soon met up with Katrina and her mom. Katrina's mom said Katrina could go on without her as long as she stayed with the "big kids." It might have been the first time in her whole life that Jessie had been called a "big kid." It made her happy. She even let Katrina loop her hand through the strap on Jessie's backpack each time they crossed a street.

"Today's the day!" shouted Katrina as she skipped alongside Jessie and David. "I hope my bridge wins. Do you think it will win, Jessie?" Katrina took an extra-high skip and bumped her hip into Jessie's hip. Jessie did not like that.

"Here's the thing, Katrina," said Jessie. She was about to explain to Katrina that her entry into the fairy camp contest for best bridge was *not* going to win. Her gluing was sloppy, her Popsicle sticks were crooked, and Jessie was pretty sure the whole thing would collapse under a load of just ten pennies.

But then David jumped in and said, "Maybe, Katrina! You might win. You never know."

"Actually. I *do* know," said Jessie. "I'm the judge." But she didn't say anything else for the rest of the walk to school.

It had been Jessie's idea to have everyone build bridges along with their fairy houses. She figured

Mrs. Richter wouldn't get any more complaints about the class being boring. Bridges were never boring. That was just a fact.

Ava had been the one to say, "Let's make it a contest!" and of course Jessie was the judge. She knew more about bridges than anyone. Even Lorelei and Andrea decided to enter the contest. Only Becky refused. "Not what I signed up for," she said, and turned her back on the other students.

Today was judging day: the last day of week two of Summer Fun Exploration Camp. Jessie couldn't believe she was already two-thirds of the way through this terrible class.

The day began with the usual Fairy Circle, which Jessie still found annoying, but not as much as she had on the first day. And the fairy tale that Pixie read to them was more interesting than most: the fairy made a bridge out of spiderwebs! Maybe the class wasn't completely terrible after all.

Everyone wanted one more look in Jessie's *Great Big Book of Bridges*, which she kept stowed in her cubby, before the judging began.

David had made a double-leaf drawbridge, which meant the decking could be raised on both sides, with a stable span in between.

Ava had made a truss bridge, using unique patterns of triangles to add strength.

Lorelei and Andrea had worked together to make a simple beam bridge. It wasn't complicated or hard to build, but Jessie was impressed with how carefully they had constructed it; not a single Popsicle stick was crooked. Not a drop of glue was visible. Also, they'd used the overlapping technique that Jessie had recommended to make the decks light but strong.

And Katrina had made a true fairy bridge that didn't fit into any category described in *The Great Big Book of Bridges*. It was covered in feathers and bedazzled with plastic gems. There were paper umbrellas lined up all the way along it so that "people won't get hot walking." She also had added a hot dog stand halfway across the bridge with one of her trolls selling hot dogs and cold drinks.

While the kids in the camp class put the finishing touches on their bridges, Jessie noticed Becky

sitting by herself. She wasn't even pretending to work. She just stared out the window. Her quartz necklace glowed in the morning light. Jessie wondered again about the shape of the pendant. She couldn't help but think that the shape meant something.

Jessie was good at matching patterns. Suddenly, the slot machine of her brain clicked into place, linking two separate images stored in her visual cortex.

She walked over to Becky. "I bet I know where your grandparents live," she said.

"I bet you don't," said Becky.

"Well, I bet I do," said Jessie. "So what do you want to bet?" Jessie liked making bets. She and Evan did it all the time.

A bet. A bet. A bet. The whispers started to circulate among the other students. David drifted over to the table where Becky and Jessie were. Lorelei and Andrea followed. Pixie was too busy at her teacher's desk, carefully combing the hair on Katrina's troll after Katrina accidentally stuck gum in it.

Becky looked at Jessie with disgust, as if an ant had just crawled out of her lunch box. "Okay," she said. "If you guess wrong, you have to promise me you won't come to Summer Fun Exploration Camp all of next week." She leaned back and smiled, running her fingers along the necklace so that the pendant made a shivery sound as it traveled back and forth on the metal chain.

"Fine," said Jessie, who knew she would win.

At that moment, she wanted revenge. Revenge for the purple glitter all over her first fairy house. Revenge for kicking her stool. Revenge for calling her names. But most of all, revenge for how mean Becky had been to her in second grade.

"But if I win," said Jessie, "then you have to give me your necklace."

Becky sat up so quickly, Jessie thought the delicate silver chain would snap right off her neck. "No!" she said. "It was a gift from my grandparents. It's the most important thing in the world to me."

"Okay," said Jessie. "I guess you're stuck with me for all of next week."

"That was a bad bet," said David to Jessie as she walked back to her seat at the other table. "You're lucky she let you off."

"It was a good bet," said Jessie, "because I would have won."

Meanwhile, Lorelei and Andrea had been whispering with Becky. Andrea walked over to Jessie. "She says she'll take the bet."

Jessie smiled and walked back over to Becky, and all the kids followed, even Katrina. Pixie glanced up from her desk, but the students were quiet, so she bent her head to the messy task of removing the gum.

"One guess," said Becky. "And it can't be a guess like 'the United States' or 'the world.'"

"I'll tell you the state," said Jessie. "Fair?"

Becky nodded.

"Wait a minute," said David. "How do we know that you'll be honest if Jessie guesses right?"

Becky reached for a scrap of fairy paper, which

was really just old wrapping paper that Pixie had recycled. "I'll write it down." She turned her back and wrote something on the paper then folded it in half and then in half again. "Make your guess."

"It's not a guess," said Jessie. "I know it for a fact." This felt like the old fairy tale "Rumpel-stiltskin" that Jessie's mother had read to her when she was little. Jessie had never liked fairy tales, but she found it fascinating that the imp had stamped his foot so hard when the queen guessed his name that he had disappeared right into the ground and was never seen again. Jessie imagined Becky doing the same thing: disappearing into the ground and never being seen again.

"Your grandparents live in Pennsylvania," said Jessie. She put out her hand, waiting for the necklace.

David snatched up the scrap of paper and read it. "She's right. Jessie won the bet."

"How did you know that?" asked Becky. Her face had gone very pale and her mouth hung slightly open. Jessie was surprised how different she looked, as if Becky had changed from one thing into another.

"Because I finally figured out what that shape is," she said, pointing at the rose quartz pendant. "It's a *keystone*, which is the top stone in a Roman arch bridge that holds the whole arch together. And there's only one reason someone would give a keystone necklace, and that's if they live in Pennsylvania, because Pennsylvania is the Keystone State."

"How do you *know* that?" asked Lorelei.

Last summer, Jessie had memorized all the states and their capitals, along with their mottos, their nicknames, their state birds, and their state flowers. Pennsylvania. Harrisburg. "Virtue, liberty, and independence." The Keystone State. The ruffed grouse. The mountain laurel.

But all she said was "I know a lot of stuff."

"Wow," said David.

With shaking hands, Becky unlooped the necklace from her neck and put it in Jessie's outstretched hand.

"Back to work, little fairies!" called Pixie from

across the room, holding Katrina's troll aloft to show off its new punk haircut. Becky asked Pixie if she could go to the bathroom, then left the room.

"Are you going to wear it?" asked David as he and Jessie walked back to their seats.

"Nah," said Jessie, shoving it in her pocket. "I hate necklaces. They make my neck feel itchy."

"So why did you make it the prize?" asked David.

Jessie shrugged, but she knew the answer. She had figured out that losing the necklace was the thing that would hurt Becky the most. So that's what Jessie set out to do: take the necklace away from Becky. And Jessie had won, so she should feel happy. But instead she felt yucky. Even with the prize safely in her pocket.

Jessie noticed that when Becky came back from the bathroom, her eyes were red and puffy.

I won it, fair and square, Jessie told herself. But that didn't help the yucky feeling go away. *I'll talk to Evan when I get home*, she thought. *He'll explain it to me.*

CHAPTER 10
FRIDAY #2

"Hi, Evan," said Miss Dixon, glancing up from the table in her office as Evan walked in. "Your shoes are untied." She pointed with her pencil.

"Oh, yeah," said Evan, sitting down opposite her. "I'll tie them later."

"There's time for you to tie your shoes before we start," said Miss Dixon. "Our schedule isn't *that* tight."

Evan hesitated, then reached down and fiddled with the laces, not really tying them, but stuffing the long ends into his shoes. Walking in shoes that were untied was proving difficult, but Evan was determined to make it through the day. He slouched in his chair.

"Sit up, sit up," said Miss Dixon kindly. "You can't concentrate with a mushy spine." She placed the last magnetic tile on the metal board in front of him, and they began to run through the drills: Single letter. Evan tapped the tile once. Say the letter, tap, make the sound. Two letters that blend together. Say the letters, tap, make the sound. Single letter plus one ending. Two taps. Sound out the word: "b," *tap*, "est," *tap*, "best"; "ch," *tap*, "ip," *tap*, "chip."

Real words. *Fall, slam, brake*. Nonsense words. *Sool, crisk, laft*. Words Evan knew and words he didn't.

The point was to be *quick*. Keep moving through the letters. Keep moving as the tiles lined up, words appearing and disappearing. Miss Dixon's hands never rested, arranging and rearranging the metal tiles, and each time, a satisfying *click* as the tile snapped into place. Evan's fingers never rested, tapping the tiles. Make a mistake. Keep moving. Circle back. Get it right this time. Keep moving. Keep moving. *Tap. Tap. Tap.*

Evan was used to drills. He did them in basketball all the time. Passing drills. Layup drills. Free-throw drills. He knew how they worked. You did one thing over and over again until your body knew how to do it without even thinking. The same was true with these drills. Miss Dixon had promised him that if he drilled enough with the metal tiles, he'd be able to read out loud in class just like the other kids.

"You're slumping again," said Miss Dixon, leaning over to where Evan's head was practically resting on the top of the table. She caught sight of his shoes, still untied, but didn't say anything. Evan pulled both feet under the table, ashamed, as if he'd been caught in a lie.

They continued tapping the metal tiles, but Evan had a hard time concentrating. He kept looking at the clock, until finally, exasperated, Miss Dixon said, "Well, go then," and waved him to the door. Miss Dixon was a good teacher—patient, kind, funny. But even *she* had her limits on a hot summer day.

Evan took off so fast, he almost lost a shoe.

If anyone had told Evan after the Frisbee-on-the-roof incident that Reed was going to *welcome* Evan into his circle of friends, Evan would have said, "You're nuts. That kid hates me. And I hate him."

But Evan was coming to realize that friendships in middle school were different from friendships in elementary school. In middle school, it was more like a battle strategy. It was more like *World of Warcraft*: alliances were formed, alliances shifted. People were thrown out of the circle, and that made room for others to join.

That Monday morning after the Frisbee-on-the-roof incident, Evan had realized that Puke was out, although no one said why, and Reed was making a big deal out of including Evan in the group. Maybe just to make Puke feel extra bad for what he'd done. Reed even shortened Evan's nickname to Goose, which sounded all right, maybe even a little cool. There'd been a famous baseball pitcher for the New York Yankees nicknamed Goose, so that was okay with Evan.

All day, and the next and the next, Reed had gone out of his way to joke around with Evan, in a nice way. He'd invited Evan to come with them to the soccer nets during their outdoor break and even told Twitch to move over so Evan could hang next to him.

Evan didn't know what to make of it, but there was one thing he was sure of: It was way better to be on Reed's good side than to be on his bad side. Suddenly, all the teasing, all the shoving, all the out-of-nowhere tripping and nonstop name-calling . . . stopped. Instead, there were invitations to get pizza after school, to stop at the drugstore to buy some candy, to hang out on the field throwing the faded orange Frisbee around.

Evan didn't understand it, but he knew a good deal when he saw one. Or at least a better deal. He stared across the playing field at Stevie sitting all by himself at the picnic table with his back turned and his shoulders hunched over. *I'm so glad that's not me*, thought Evan.

And maybe Reed wasn't a completely bad guy. Well. Evan knew he wasn't a *good* guy. He was never someone Evan would be friends with in his regular life. But summer school with older kids was anything but regular. It was a strange, confusing world, and Evan felt off-balance, as if he was dribbling up court and suddenly all the other players were wearing different-colored jerseys. Who were his teammates? Who could he trust?

For the moment, his teammate was Reed. For better or for worse.

After school, they all stopped at the drugstore on the way to the park—Evan and Reed and Frank and Twitch. Reed wanted to get some gummy bears. They were his favorite. Evan had a five-dollar bill in his pocket that he'd been saving for more than a month now for the next edition of his favorite comic book series, *Razorman*. Looking at the comics on display, he saw that the new issue wasn't out yet. He would save his money. The comic might be released tomorrow or maybe the day after.

He was flipping through *The Red Hornet* when Reed and the other two came up to him. Reed leaned in and whispered, "We're all stealing something. Doesn't matter what. But you gotta do it."

"He'll never do it," said Frank. Twitch laughed.

"He'll do it," said Reed quietly. And as Frank and Twitch headed for the door, Reed whispered, "Don't mess this up, Goose Boy. We're watching you." And just like that, Evan saw how quickly it could all go back to the way it was. He would be Stevie again, sitting at the picnic table.

Evan had never stolen anything in his life. Not from a store, not from a friend. That was real stealing. Yeah, sometimes he would sneak the last french fry off Jessie's plate if she wasn't looking, and sometimes he and his friends would swipe each other's shoes or something, just for a laugh. One time he'd found a dollar bill stuck inside a library book, and he'd kept it. He never even told his mother. Was that stealing or was that the rule of finders keepers?

But he had never shoplifted anything from a store. That wasn't who he was, and he knew it. He didn't need his mother telling him it was wrong. He knew it, right down to his bones.

We're watching you. And they were. Evan could see all three of them through the large plate glass window that ran along the front of the store. Reed and Frank and Twitch were standing on the sidewalk, just outside the door. The cashier was posted like a sentry between them.

Evan walked slowly down the aisle of candy bins. Which one would be the easiest to pick up? He kept his hands down by his side, like he was ready to receive a low bounce pass, and continued to walk toward the cashier. He glanced out the window. Reed was staring at him. Daring him. Daring him to steal. Daring him to fail.

Evan scooped up a king-size Almond Joy and held it close to his leg, hidden from the view of the cashier. She was old, with pink lipstick and gray hair pulled back in a stub of a ponytail. He started to head for the door, knowing he'd have to walk right in front of the checkout counter, smile, meet her eyes, act like nothing was going on. Evan wondered what Jessie would think of what he was doing. His timing would have to be just right. He slowed his walk, keeping his eyes on Reed.

And then there was the noise of a dog barking outside, and all three boys looked across the street for a second. Just a second. Evan flashed the candy bar at the cashier and tossed his five-dollar bill on the counter, all in one fluid motion. Like the perfect layup. "Just this," he said, stuffing the candy bar in his pocket, never breaking his stride, heading for the door.

"It doesn't cost that much!" she said. "You've got change!"

But Evan didn't stop. He walked out the door and said to Reed, "Let's get out of here," and all four boys hurried through the parking lot and jumped over the low fence that put them one street over.

After showing the candy bar to Reed and the others to prove he had swiped it, he didn't eat it. It rested in the side pocket of his cargo shorts, a slight weight that set his whole frame off-balance. He would never eat it. He knew that. Just knowing it was in his pocket made him feel sick.

CHAPTER 11
TENSION AND COMPRESSION

"Why are you so late?" asked Jessie. Evan was supposed to get home an hour and ten minutes after she did, but he had been late every day this week. She was tired of waiting. She had to talk to him.

"I'm not late for dinner," said Evan.

"You're late for talking to *me*," said Jessie impatiently. "I need to talk to you, and I've been waiting for *two and three-quarters* hours."

"Well, sor-ry," said Evan. "It's been kind of a rotten week. And believe it or not, Jess, sometimes I don't spend all day thinking about *you*."

Jessie narrowed her eyes and looked at her brother's face. She was pretty sure this was an example of *sarcasm*. Sarcasm was when someone said one thing but meant exactly the opposite! Who invented such a thing? That's what Jessie wanted to know. Jessie needed people to say exactly what they meant, or else she was lost. She always said exactly what she meant. Why couldn't everyone else be like her? It would make life so much easier.

But then she thought that she *didn't* want Evan to be just like her. She needed him to be just like him! Otherwise, how could she find out if someone was being sarcastic if she didn't have Evan to ask?

"Are you being sarcastic?" she asked.

"Yeah," said Evan, getting up to get a yogurt from the refrigerator. And this time, he sounded more like himself. "Sorry. For real. I just had a rotten day."

Jessie was about to tell him it was too close to dinnertime to eat a yogurt, but then she bit her tongue, which was a trick her mother had taught her for when she *wanted* to correct someone but didn't *need* to correct someone. It was a difficult distinction to spot. In this case, she had to bite her tongue twice.

"It's okay," she said. "I have a problem. A problem at Summer Fun Exploration Camp."

"Are those girls being mean to you?" asked Evan.

"No!" said Jessie. "I think *I'm* being mean to them. At least to one of them. The other two kind of like me now. For no good reason. Which is even stranger than when they didn't like me, also for no good reason."

"I don't know what you're talking about," said Evan, scooping a spoonful of yogurt into his mouth. Evan could finish a yogurt in five scoops. Jessie had counted. It made her kind of sick. Yogurt was slimy and cold. Like eating a raw egg. Or a slug.

"I will explain," said Jessie. And she told him the whole story of the bet with Becky and how she had won, but how it hadn't felt good. Not like when she'd won the Lemonade War against Evan, which he *still* claimed was a tie, even though *it was not*. "It feels like I did something bad," said Jessie. "But I didn't! I won, fair and square."

"Well, I wouldn't call it fair and square," said Evan, putting the yogurt container in the recycling bin. "The problem is, Jess, you're ten times smarter than Becky. For Pete's sake, you're ten times smarter than just about anybody. So it's never really going to be fair and square with you. You always start with a serious advantage."

"That's not my fault!" said Jessie. This conversation was not helping her at all.

"Nope," said Evan. "It's not your fault. It's just something you gotta remember. Because you've got an edge—which is great. You just gotta think about how you use it, right?" He rinsed the spoon and put it in the dishwasher. "Can I see the necklace?"

Jessie reached into her pocket and put the necklace on the kitchen counter. Evan picked it up and looked at the rose quartz stone.

"What did you say this thing was called?" he asked.

"A keystone," said Jessie. She grabbed a piece of

scrap paper and the pencil from the special holder on the refrigerator. "It's the top stone in an arch bridge." She drew a picture. "You make other stones exactly the same size and weight, and then you put the keystone at the top, and the whole bridge holds together, without any cement or glue or anything."

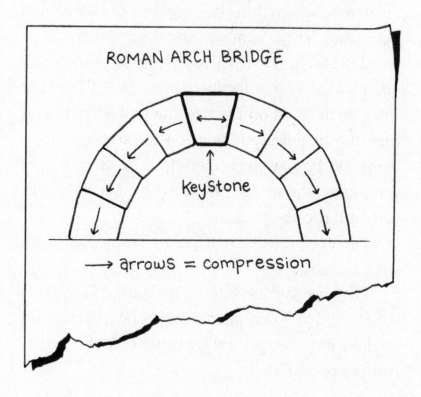

ROMAN ARCH BRIDGE

Keystone

→ arrows = compression

"There's no way that thing holds together without cement," said Evan.

"It does!" said Jessie. This was one of the things she loved about bridges. The way they used invisible scientific forces, like gravity and tension and compression, to carry impossible loads. It was almost like magic. "The Romans built an arch bridge in Spain without anything holding the stones together. Each stone weighs *eight tons*, and the bridge has been standing for more than *two thousand* years." She quickly added some arrows to her sketch. "The keystone pushes out on the two stones next to it, and then those stones push out on the stones next to them, all the way to the bottom. The more weight you put on the bridge, the *stronger* it becomes. But you need the keystone."

"I don't believe it," said Evan. "Things just don't work like that."

"I'll show you!" said Jessie defiantly. "I'll make a model, and you can put the keystone in place and see how it stays together. We can even put a load of pennies on top!"

Evan sighed. "Whatever. I've got bigger things to worry about." He looked out the window into the backyard, and Jessie knew he was thinking about the Climbing Tree. It was gone. But the Climbing Tree used to be the place that Evan would go when something was bothering him and he had to think it out. The tree had come down in a hurricane last month. Jessie missed it too, but not like Evan.

"What's in your pocket?" asked Jessie.

"Huh?" said Evan. He stiffened up.

"There's something crinkly in there," she said. "I can hear it every time you move."

Evan looked at her, and Jessie had *no* idea what kind of face *that* was. Mad? Surprised? Relieved? All three? Who knew!

Evan pulled his hand out of his pocket and dropped a giant Almond Joy on the countertop, right next to the necklace.

Jessie made a face. "I hate those."

"So do I," said Evan.

"No you don't," said Jessie. "That's your *third* favorite candy bar, after Reese's Peanut Butter Cups and Milky Ways. Although, technically, a peanut butter cup is *not* a candy bar. It's a cup. It should be in its own category."

"You can have it," said Evan, pushing the Almond Joy across the counter toward her.

Jessie pushed it back. "I don't want it. You know they make me throw up. Why don't *you* want it?"

Evan looked glumly at the candy bar and muttered, "Because I pretended to steal it from the drugstore today, and I'm mad at myself for being such an idiot."

"You stole candy!" shrieked Jessie. To her, stealing was just about the biggest lie a person could tell. Jessie hated dishonesty of all kinds. Even sarcasm was a kind of dishonesty, in her opinion. But this was bigger! Evan *stole* a candy bar?

"I didn't!" said Evan hotly. "I paid for it. I paid, like, five times what that thing costs."

"You mean your comic book money? The five dollars you saved?" Jessie had helped Evan save that money by keeping it for him in her lockbox so he couldn't spend it. Jessie was really good at saving money. Evan, not so much. "Why did you spend five dollars to buy your third-favorite candy bar?"

"I don't even know," said Evan. "It's just . . . I can't stand it when other kids . . . don't . . . when they . . . I don't like being the one on the outside."

"What?" asked Jessie. "You love being outside. You spend all your time outside."

"I don't mean outside, like—" Evan waved his hands toward the window. "Out-*side*. I mean when everyone is a group and they hang out together, but you're not part of that group. You're . . . separate. And alone."

"Oh," said Jessie. She thought about that for a minute, but it was impossible for her to imagine Evan on the outside. He had so many friends, and people always liked him. Always. His teachers called him a natural-born leader. How could a leader be on the outside? It didn't make sense to her. "I think you're confused," she said. "You're never on the outside. You're the one at the top. You're the keystone."

"Maybe I used to be," muttered Evan. "Not this

summer. This summer, I'm just some dumb Goose Boy who has to go to school because he's a lousy reader who can't do math."

"Goose Boy? What are you even talking about?" Jessie could feel her head starting to spin. She didn't like it when Evan looked sad and confused. He was her big brother who always had the answers, who always helped her when she couldn't figure things out on her own. If he was confused, what chance did she have? Jessie could feel her insides bubble up and words start to spill out of her mouth. "Goose Boy! I hate geese. They poop!"

"Never mind," said Evan, scooping up the candy bar and putting it in the trash. "I'll figure it out. The worst is probably over anyway." He looked around the kitchen. "What's for dinner?"

"Pizza!" said Jessie excitedly. "Mom's on deadline and she said we could order any large pizza, but just one for the two of us to share. Please can it be plain cheese? Please?" Evan liked all kinds of disgusting things on pizza, like pepperoni and onions and even mushrooms. Mushrooms were a fungus!

Why would anyone want to eat a fungus? Jessie liked pizzas that were simple. And plain cheese was as simple as you could get.

"Sure," said Evan. "Cheese is fine."

That was strange. Evan usually argued about pizza toppings. In the end, they always went half and half, but Jessie didn't like that either, because sometimes a fungus would land on her half.

Jessie watched her brother as he went upstairs. Then she got out her model clay and started to mold six shapes that were the same size as the keystone on the necklace. She hummed while she worked. She was sure a demonstration of an arch bridge would cheer Evan up.

CHAPTER 12
JUST A JOKE

Puke had gone in to see the nurse because he'd scraped his elbow on the blacktop and it needed to get cleaned up. Evan would remember that later. It had all started when Puke went inside to see the nurse.

It was Tuesday, the third week of summer school. Evan hoped that the worst was over. He'd proven himself to Reed and the others by "stealing" the candy bar. Maybe now things would settle down and they could all just hang out.

But Evan was exhausted. He'd never realized how hard it was to fit in when you didn't. How much work it was to laugh at jokes that weren't funny or look the other way when Reed was mean to Stevie or one of the other kids.

At least Reed wasn't mean to Evan, and that counted for something.

Or so he thought.

"Hey," said Reed, getting that crooked smile on his face that meant he was about to do something he wasn't supposed to. "Let's play a joke on Puke."

Puke hadn't been let back into the group, and Evan still didn't understand why, but he knew enough not to ask questions. Questions made Reed mad. And that was never fun.

"Yeah," said Twitch. "Let's do something to Puke."

Evan allowed himself to drift a couple of steps away from the group, hoping that somehow he wouldn't be included. Maybe if he just kept drifting, a little more, a little more, they wouldn't notice, and he wouldn't have to be part of the joke, which he knew was going to be a little bit funny but mostly mean.

Reed was already scooping pebbles from the ground into a large empty Skittles bag. He twisted the top and handed it to Evan. "Here," he said. "You take these and go up on the roof, and then when Puke walks out, I'll give you the signal, and you drop them on his head." He exploded his hands over his own head, as if a shower of pebbles had landed on him, and started laughing. Of course, Frank and Twitch laughed too.

Evan smiled but shook his head. "I'm not going on the roof. I'll get in trouble."

Frank and Twitch started to tease him for being afraid, mimicking the way he had said *I'll get in trouble,* but Reed just crossed his arms and scowled at him. "You're no fun," he finally said, and turned his back on Evan.

"If I go on the roof, they'll kick me out of summer school," said Evan.

"Only if they catch you," said Reed, "and how

would that happen? You'll only be up there for, like, a minute."

"So why don't you do it?" asked Evan.

"Because I'm the signal man, which is a whole lot more complicated than climbing on the roof and dumping a bag of rocks."

"Well, why can't Frank do it? Or Twitch?" Evan knew he sounded scared, and that wasn't allowed. There was nothing cool about being scared.

Reed shrugged. "They can," he said. "That's the difference."

Evan heard the boys whispering, but the only word he could hear was "fifth-grader." They all laughed. Evan hated feeling this way. He felt ashamed, not because of anything he had done, but just because of who he was. A kid who wouldn't climb on the roof to dump a bunch of rocks on another kid's head. *Natural-born leader.* Instead, he felt like a natural-born loser.

"Let's go," said Reed. They all started to move toward the school, but Reed pivoted and said to

Evan, "Not you." Then he continued to walk, waving the Skittles bag over his head and calling out, "We don't need you anymore."

Evan stopped walking, but the rest of his body leaned toward the retreating group. The urge to follow, to be a part of something, to belong, was more than Evan could resist.

"Okay, I'll do it," said Evan, surprising himself. It was just a stupid joke. It wouldn't hurt anyone. Puke would pretend to think it was funny. He might even be happy about it. After all, you don't joke around with someone who's not in the group. And Puke wanted to find his way back in. Maybe Evan was just helping Puke get what he wanted.

They looked at the flat part of the roof that covered the door where Puke would come out. Evan wouldn't be able to see him coming, so he needed someone to signal him to dump the pebbles. In the end, it was Frank who would give the signal, with Reed standing a safe distance away, where he could see it all. The whole joke depended on Frank giving the signal at exactly the right instant and Evan having quick reflexes so that the shower of pebbles would hit the mark. Too early or too late, and the joke wouldn't work.

Evan liked the complexity of the maneuvers. It was like running a well-designed pattern play in basketball. Everyone had a job to do. Everyone had to be in the right place at the right time. He liked the teamwork, too. He hoped Puke would think it was funny and that Evan would be able to scramble off the roof before an adult noticed what was going on. Puke could be counted on not to shout or call attention to the joke. He'd be a good sport about it. Reed would make sure of that.

Twitch handed Evan the Skittles bag with the pebbles in it, the top twisted shut so none of the rocks would spill out. Later, Evan would wonder why he hadn't noticed that the bag felt lighter than it should have. But at the time, he didn't think twice. He was too busy worrying about being on the roof.

Getting up was easy, the way it had been last time. Evan crept low, keeping away from the edges, and scrambled the last six feet on his stomach. His mother would wonder why his T-shirt was so dusty and dirty, and for a second Evan thought about what he was doing and what his mother would think about it. She had always told him, "Character is what you do when you know no one is looking." But everyone was looking. All the time. And Evan was exhausted by it. He really hoped Puke would laugh. Maybe it would be something like getting a bucket full of ice water dumped on your head to celebrate a big win—shocking, but fun.

Evan lay on his stomach, his head low to the rooftop, his hands reaching over the edge. He could just see Frank in position. He untwisted the bag, ready to empty its contents. Later, he would be angry with himself: He noticed the smell, but didn't think through what it meant.

Frank gave him the pre-signal: a raised arm. Evan watched and waited, the bag held in his outstretched hand, poised over the edge. It was only a couple of seconds before Frank swooped his arm through the air, like a Nascar official waving the winning flag in a race. Evan flipped the bag over and the contents spilled out.

Right away, Evan knew something was wrong. Whatever was in the bag didn't feel like pebbles spilling out and it definitely didn't smell like pebbles. It smelled horrible. The stuff rolled out of the bag like spongy clods of something, leaving a trail of pure stink.

Evan just barely caught sight of Reed, with Frank and Twitch and Puke, all laughing as they hurried to the far side of the field. Evan scrambled to look over the edge of the roof—to see what he had done.

Stevie stared up at him. He was covered in goose poop. It hadn't been pebbles inside the bag at all. At some point, Reed had switched bags. The green, grassy poop was in Stevie's hair, resting on his shoulders, falling into the pocket on his T-shirt. He stared at Evan, and Evan stared back at him, both of them confused and horrified.

Evan scrambled away from the edge of the roof. He had to get down. He had to get away from the roof. He had to hide until he could figure out what had happened. How had this happened? This wasn't a joke at all. It was a mean, rotten, lousy thing to do. And *he* had done it to Stevie. But Reed had done it to *Evan*.

Reed had gotten them both. When it came to being mean, Reed was the keystone.

CHAPTER 13
WHERE IS PIXIE?

Jessie woke up on Thursday knowing that everything was going to go wrong that day.

Maybe it was because Evan had stayed home sick from school yesterday, and Evan was never sick. Plus, he'd put up the Locked sign on his door and stayed in his room even through meals, which wasn't allowed unless you were sick.

Maybe it was because their mother had asked Jessie if she knew what was going on with Evan.

Had he said anything to her? Was he upset about something? Jessie hadn't known the answer, but she didn't like the questions. They made her feel itchy-uncomfortable. Evan wasn't supposed to act like this. He wasn't doing what he was supposed to do.

Maybe she woke up in a dark mood because the keystone necklace still sat in her desk drawer and she hadn't figured out what to do with it or why it bothered her so much.

Or maybe it was because the deadline for the bridge competition was just two days away and she wasn't finished with her entry. The bridge was still in pieces, waiting to be assembled on the large art table at school. When it was finished, it would be six feet long, with two towers and a single span. But had she made the towers tall enough? Had she made the cables strong enough and were there enough of them? Would the bridge hold her weight, which was the whole point of her entry?

She stood up to make her bed. Making her bed always calmed her down.

* * *

"Jessie!" shouted Katrina from across the classroom as soon as Jessie walked in. "Pixie is gone!"

Jessie thought Katrina meant that Pixie had gone to the bathroom.

But Katrina kept talking. "No one knows where she is, but some old lady is here this morning. And she isn't wearing wings! And she doesn't know the fairy song! And she isn't Pixie!" Katrina's eyes began to swim with tears, and Jessie worried that she would have a full-on kindergarten gusher on her hands if she didn't do something to stop it.

"Katrina," said Jessie, "I think you're wrong. Pixie would never leave us like that."

"She didn't leave," said Becky in a harsh voice. "She got kicked out. Because she's a crummy teacher. And that's what happens when you're no good. You get kicked out."

"Well, if Pixie's gone, who's the teacher?" asked Jessie. There were still two days left of Summer Fun Exploration Camp, and she needed both days to work on her suspension bridge for the contest. The due date for entering was Saturday.

"Well, I suppose this is *everybody*," said a voice so heavy and discouraged you would think the person speaking those words was carrying an elephant on her back. Jessie turned to look at the teacher standing in the doorway.

"Mrs. Feeney?" said Jessie. *Oh! The horror!* Mrs. Feeney was the world's worst substitute teacher. Everybody in the whole school knew that. She was grouchy and despondent. She never bothered to learn anyone's name. And last year, when she had substituted in Jessie and Evan's fourth grade class, she had spent most of the day checking her phone. She was the worst.

"Yes, it's me," said Mrs. Feeney. "And I'm here for the rest of the week, so we'll all just have to make the best of it."

"But where is Pixie?" asked Jessie.

"Who?" Mrs. Feeney was already glancing at the screen on her phone. She shook her head and frowned as she shoved the phone back into the pocket of her pants.

"Our teacher," said Jessie. She was surprised that she was calling Pixie that, since Jessie had always had her doubts about whether Pixie was a *real* teacher.

"Amanda? Amanda Osborne?"

Everyone in the classroom grew quiet. "Was that her name?" asked David.

Jessie suddenly realized that of course her name wasn't really Pixie. No one names a child Pixie! She had been lying to them. Pretending to be someone she wasn't. Jessie felt a stab in her heart as she thought about the falseness of the name and wondered what else Pixie had lied about.

"She changed her name to Amanda?" asked Katrina. "Why would she do that? Pixie is so much better!"

"No!" said Jessie, exasperated. "It's not her name. Her real name—"

"Jessie!" said David. "Let's not . . . worry too much about names right now."

"How that girl got to be teaching a class is

beyond me," said Mrs. Feeney. "She certainly wasn't a *model* student, I can tell you that. Never paid attention in class and always caused trouble of one kind or another."

Katrina started to cry.

"That isn't a correct statement," said Jessie. "You're using anecdotal evidence to reach a conclusion."

"Excuse me?" said Mrs. Feeney.

"You would need to collect data on Pixie to reach a conclusion about her. You can't just use your own personal memories. That isn't science! Maybe she was a great student on the days when you weren't there. A lot of kids misbehave when a substitute teacher is around."

"Tell me something I don't know!" said Mrs. Feeney, waving both hands in disgust and turning to the teacher's desk, where Pixie kept her attendance list.

"This is a Day of Misery," said Jessie to David, remembering the term that she and Evan used when things were going particularly badly at home.

"Katrina, I think it would be best if you stopped crying."

Surprisingly, Katrina did. She turned her tear-stained face to Jessie with a look of hope and expectation. David did too, as if they were both waiting for her to say something or do something. In fact, everyone in the class was looking at her, except for Becky, who was scowling in the corner.

What did they expect from her? She was just as disappointed as they were that Pixie was gone.

Mrs. Feeney made a puffing sound of resignation. "I can't understand these notes she left. *I* don't know these songs or dances. And how am I supposed to read *Thumbelina* when there's no book?"

Jessie felt herself getting angry. This was just like last year when Mrs. Feeney had substituted for Mrs. Overton and given up on teaching the poetry lesson because, she had said, she was "just not a poetry person."

Jessie supposed Mrs. Feeney wasn't a "fairy person," either. Well, neither was Jessie, but she wasn't going to give up! Jessie did not like quitters. And she didn't like Mrs. Feeney.

"*We* know all the songs. And all the dances, too," said Jessie. "C'mon, Katrina. You start the Jig of the Highland Fairies and we'll join in."

Katrina was so pleased to be the leader that she forgot all about crying. Soon, everyone in the class was dancing and clapping their hands, except for Becky, who had asked to be excused to go to the bathroom, and Mrs. Feeney, who was staring at her phone screen from behind the teacher's desk.

After lunch when they were returning their empty lunch bags to their cubbies in the hallway, Jessie walked up to Becky and asked, "Did you get Pixie fired?"

"That's a dumb thing to say," said Becky. "How could I get someone fired?"

"If you complained to your mom and she complained to Mrs. Richter."

Becky rolled her eyes and let out an impatient puff of air. "I'm allowed to say whatever I want to my mother. And I told her the truth. So what? This class is the worst class ever, and Pixie—or whoever she is—is a terrible teacher. She has no idea what she's doing."

"Pixie was doing her best, and everyone else thought the class was pretty fun. Even Lorelei and Andrea liked it."

"They did not! They're *my* friends."

"Who said anything about friends?" asked Jessie. "I'm just saying they were having fun."

"With what? Fairy houses? Or making bridges?" asked Becky, and Jessie could not understand why she was getting so jumpy mad. "This was supposed to be a class about fairy houses. That's what we were promised. And then you turned it into making bridges, which is *not* what any of us signed up for! You can't just go switching the class like that! It's not allowed! And also, it isn't fair that you took my necklace away from me. That was a trick. I should tell my mother to tell your mother that you took it away from me and I want it back!"

Jessie was completely confused by all the angry things that were tumbling out of Becky, one right after the other. Was she angry that they *weren't* building fairy houses or that they *were* building bridges? Was she mad that the class hadn't turned out to be what she wanted? Or that Lorelei and Andrea weren't following Becky like they usually did? Or was it, in the end, just that she wanted her necklace back? The necklace that Jessie had left in her desk drawer at home because she didn't even care about it?

"Stop saying so many things at once!" said Jessie. "I can't figure out what you're really upset about."

"Well, that's not my problem," said Becky, shoving her lunch bag in her cubby and turning to walk back into the classroom. "And it's not my fault that Pixie got fired. She deserved it." Then she disappeared through the classroom door.

David drifted over. "I heard all that," he said. "Wow, she's really mad. I just can't believe she got Pixie fired. She wasn't the best teacher, but she wasn't the worst."

"Mrs. Feeney is the worst," said Jessie. "We won't learn anything the rest of the week. She'll just let us do whatever we want."

"That's good for you!" said David brightly. "You can finish the suspension bridge for the contest. And I can help you!"

"I suppose," said Jessie. She should have been happy. But Jessie would miss Pixie wandering over and asking questions about how her bridge worked. Or telling Jessie she was a very smart fairy. Jessie would even miss the fairy songs, which were pretty and soothing, though she wouldn't miss the dancing. That had been ridiculous.

Jessie would miss Pixie. What an unexpected outcome.

"Hey, can you show me the picture of the Dinosaur Bridge in Tokyo?" asked David. "I want to try to build one like that for my fairy house this week. I brought in a whole new bag of Popsicle sticks. Five hundred!"

Jessie reached for the *The Great Big Book of Bridges*,

which she kept in her cubby. It felt oddly stiff and heavy as she picked it up, and she knew why, the second she tried to open it.

Every single page was glued shut.

Someone had spread glue on each page and then closed the book so that it would dry into a heavy block. And they had done it very carefully, because there wasn't a single drop of glue on the outside. To look at it, you would think the book was just fine. But it was ruined.

An unexpected outcome.

CHAPTER 14
YOU GET
USED TO IT

On Tuesday, Evan told his mother he was sick and spent the whole day at home, waiting for the phone to ring so that the school could tell her that Evan had been expelled. It was going to be awful no matter what, but he'd rather get the news when he was at home than have it happen in the middle of the school day. He imagined being escorted to the principal's office while Reed and his gang smirked as he passed, delighted by the success of their double prank: they'd nailed Stevie *and* Evan, all in one mean joke. Two birds, one stone. Two sitting ducks. Or geese, like Reed had said.

But the phone didn't ring and his mother didn't say anything on Tuesday, except to ask him what was wrong. Evan said nothing was wrong, but he stayed home sick on Wednesday too.

So now Evan was walking to school on Thursday, confused that he hadn't been expelled, but expecting the worst when he arrived. The first thing Evan learned when he reached the school was that someone had destroyed one of the goose nests— smashed all the eggs inside it and scattered the nest all over the wetlands. And now there were two geese, a mated pair, wandering forlornly around the playground as if they couldn't remember what they were doing there.

"Will they build another nest?" asked Lucy— the nice girl who had told Evan about Stevie falling down the concrete steps. She was talking to another girl on the playground, but Evan could hear.

"I don't know," said the girl. "Isn't it kind of late

for them to start over? They look so sad and confused."

If the geese were confused, Evan was even more so. He didn't understand why he wasn't expelled. Stevie had *seen* him. Their eyes had met over the edge of the roof. He must have told someone.

In the classroom, Evan watched Mrs. Warner, who was talking casually to another teacher as her students settled into their seats. She didn't look like she was about to expel Evan.

Then Evan noticed that Stevie's seat was empty. He leaned across the aisle to Lucy. "Hey!" he whispered. "Where's Stevie?"

"Not sure. He was out yesterday, too," she said. "I think he hurt his wrist. Or his elbow. Someone said he had to go to the hospital. That kid has the worst luck."

Luck. If only it were a matter of luck.

"Evan?" Evan's head snapped back to the front of the classroom, and he looked at Mrs. Warner. This was it.

She air-tapped her pencil in the direction of the clock on the wall. "You meet at nine with Miss Dixon, yes?"

"Oh, yeah," said Evan, picking up his backpack. He hurried to the door, ignoring the low-level laughing. He couldn't tell if it was just Reed and his friends or the whole class. At this point, it didn't matter. It felt like the whole world was laughing at him.

"Shoelaces tied? Both shoes!" said Miss Dixon with an approving grin. "Glad to see you're back, Evan."

"Huh?" He dropped his backpack next to the chair and sat down.

"You were out yesterday," said Miss Dixon, lining up the tiles.

"Oh, right. I thought you meant something else."

"Maybe I did!" said Miss Dixon, smiling mischievously. "Shoelaces can say a lot about a person. Let's begin with the digraphs, okay? Just to mix it up a little."

"Miss Dixon," said Evan. He pushed his chair back so there was more room between him and the table, and his shoulders slumped a little. "Is this doing any good?"

"What? The reading program?"

"Yeah, because I don't feel like it is. Every day, it's the same thing. I tap the tiles and make the sounds, but what has it got to do with reading?" He was thinking about how he felt when he was called on to read aloud in class. The slow, halting sounds he made, when other kids his age could just read as if they were talking. He was thinking of all his mistakes. And not just the ones he made when he was reading. *Was* he getting any better?

"Let me show you," said Miss Dixon, opening her three-ring notebook that had Evan's name on it. "Let's look at this. You see, every day that we work together I fill in this chart with *all* these different numbers. They're different metrics, which just means things I count—repeats, substituted sounds, missed sounds, and so on—and then I take all those metrics, all those numbers, and I make a graph of your progress. And here it is." She pulled out an accordion-folded piece of paper that was as long as her arm and showed him the lines on it. "These show your progress in every metric, and in every single one, you're improving. Every one. I have no reason to believe that you won't continue to make progress all the way through the eight weeks that we work together. And I've already put in the paperwork so we can work together for all of next year. So, I would say that by the end of fifth grade, before you go to middle school, you'll be at or above reading grade level."

Evan looked at the graphs. The lines did all go up. But somehow it didn't make him feel better. What did it matter if the lines went up? He could still hear the echo of the laughter as he left the classroom.

"You don't look convinced," said Miss Dixon.

Evan shrugged. He didn't want to hurt Miss Dixon's feelings.

"Okay," she said. "We're really not supposed to

do this, so don't tell anyone or I'll get in trouble." Again, she had that mischievous smile on her face. "Let's go freestyle."

She told Evan to pick a book off the shelf—she had hundreds of kids' books in her office—and open it to any page and pick any paragraph and read it out loud.

"In the middle?" he asked. "But I won't know what's going on or the names or anything about the story." He felt himself tense up. Evan needed to start a book slowly. Usually, he read the first page twice, just so he could figure out what was going on and who was who. If he started in the middle, he'd be completely lost.

"Evan, you've been practicing with nonsense words for more than two weeks. You don't need to know what's going on in the book to read the words. You'll figure it out as you go. Now, use the strategies. Break down every word. Tap the page, if you want. Do just what we've been doing, but instead of tiles, read from the book."

Evan bent his head low over the book.

"Sit up straight. That's one of our strategies, right? No mushy spines here."

Evan sat up. He opened the book and picked the shortest paragraph on the page. The first few words were easy and then he hit one he didn't know, but he tapped it out. And then he read a few more and used the tapping, but just inside his head.

"Breathe," said Miss Dixon quietly.

Evan took a breath, which gave his brain a minute to catch up with itself. He read a few more words, and then he read the next three sentences without hardly stopping at all—and that was the end of the paragraph.

Evan closed the book.

"You see?" said Miss Dixon. "Just like it says on my graphs."

Evan looked at the cover of the book, *A Wrinkle in Time*. "I didn't know I could do that."

"But you can. I will stake my life on this, Evan: You are capable of many great things if you work at them. *And* keep your spine straight. It always helps to have a backbone!" She laughed.

Evan smiled for the first time since Monday afternoon. He decided that when Stevie came back to school, he was going to talk to him as soon as he could. He was going to have a backbone—and apologize.

Thursday was a long day. With Stevie gone, Reed and his friends focused all their attention on making Evan miserable. Reed tripped him in the hallway—twice. Frank kicked his shoes and the backs of his legs as they walked to the cafeteria. And someone put a long, wriggling earthworm in his lunch bag. Not to mention the constant comments muttered in voices just low enough that Mrs. Warner couldn't hear, but loud enough that the rest of the kids laughed. After school, Evan was the first one out the classroom door. He ran the whole way home.

On Friday when Evan walked into the classroom, Stevie was in his usual seat with his left arm in a sling and his head bent down over his work. Evan noticed a couple of gummy bears on the floor around his chair. Evan went for his session with Miss Dixon, and when he came back an hour later, he saw that there was a really bad word written on Stevie's desk in permanent marker with an arrow pointing right at Stevie.

The class went outside for its fifteen-minute morning break, and Evan found Stevie at his usual spot at the picnic table on the edge of the field.

"I've been meaning to give these back to you for a week," said Evan, taking the three metal knights out of his shorts pocket and putting them on the table. He was careful to set each one on the table so that it was standing: the one with the long sword raised, the one with the club lifted over his head, and the one running at full speed. Stevie looked up at him with the most painful expression, a mixture of shock, relief, and deep humiliation.

"I think they're really cool," said Evan quickly. "I never had soldiers as good as these. Mine were plastic. One of them melted because I left it in the car on a really hot day."

He laughed, and Stevie did too.

"You didn't tell anyone, did you?" asked Evan. "That it was me. I would have been expelled by now if you had, so . . . I guess you didn't."

Stevie shook his head. "Nah, I never tell."

Evan looked at the soldiers on the table that Stevie was arranging and rearranging. "How come?"

Stevie shrugged. "Grownups don't really do much. My dad thinks I'm too sensitive, and I need to toughen up. He says it's a hard world out there and I should get used to it. I don't know. Maybe he's right. Maybe it's my fault."

"He's not right," said Evan. "Nobody deserves to be bullied." He paused for a minute, thinking about all the things that had happened over the last few weeks. "That's all Reed is. He's just a bully."

There it was. A simple statement of fact. It felt to Evan as though saying that one word out loud made Reed shrink down to half his size—made him shrink down to the size of the little soldiers standing on the picnic table.

Stevie shrugged again. Evan could tell his words weren't making any difference. After all, words weren't going to stop Reed from doing terrible things to Stevie. Why should Stevie care what Evan said?

Evan took a deep breath, then he stood up straighter. "And I was a bully, too. I'm super sorry about what I did. It was supposed to be a prank on a different kid, not you. And it was supposed to be pebbles, not goose poop. I never would have thrown goose poop on anyone. But I still shouldn't have done it, and I'm really sorry. Friends?" He stuck out his hand to shake the way his mother had taught him to do.

Stevie didn't reach out his hand. Instead, he looked across the field to where Reed and his friends were hanging on the soccer net. "They're not going to like it," said Stevie, and Evan realized that Stevie spent a big part of every day trying to game out what would make Reed angry and what would keep him away.

"*Eh*, who cares what they think?" said Evan.

"They just act mean to try to make themselves feel big."

"I wish they didn't exist," said Stevie, shifting the knights on the table as if they were chess pieces on a precise board.

"*I* wish you had more knights," said Evan, "so we could set up a battle."

"I actually do," said Stevie. "I have three hundred and sixty-four of them at home. But I only carry about a dozen with me." He reached into his pocket and took out a handful of the small metal soldiers.

"Don't those things stab you when you walk?" asked Evan.

"Yeah, but you get used to it," said Stevie.

Stevie looked up from the table and over Evan's shoulder and suddenly started stuffing all the knights back into his pockets as fast as he could. Evan turned around to see what had spooked him.

All the other kids on the playground had backed away.

Reed and his gang were coming straight for Evan.

CHAPTER 15
SOMETHING DIABOLICAL

"You have got to *get* her!" hissed David. It was Friday, the last day of camp.

Jessie waved her hand to make David go away, the way her mother sometimes waved a dish towel to shoo a fly in the kitchen. She was busy examining the understructure of her bridge. Was it strong enough to hold the load she had planned? Jessie imagined herself walking across the bridge and an entire auditorium full of people bursting into applause.

"So, you're just going to let her get away with it?"

asked David. "She *ruined* your book! If it was me, I'd think of something diabolical."

Jessie arched her eyebrows, never taking her eyes off her bridge. "I don't think you would. You're not the diabolical type."

"You are!" said David cheerfully. "You could think of something really great! Something that would teach her to leave you alone!"

Jessie pressed her hand firmly on the deck of the bridge. The underside stretched while the top of the bridge squeezed together. Tension and compression, in perfect balance. But would the balance hold on the day of the contest? It was only two days away. And how could she test the bridge without destroying it?

"Jessie! Someone has to make Becky stop being mean!"

"David Kirkorian!" said Jessie sharply. "Stop it! I think she's learned her lesson." Jessie looked across the room at Becky, who sat by herself, taping toilet paper tubes together. Andrea and Lorelei had joined the others to build Katrina's troll bridge.

Jessie wondered if Becky was bored or lonely or angry—or maybe all three at once. Mixed-up emotions were impossible to figure out. Jessie hated it when she felt more than one thing at a time. It was like someone had turned on a blender inside her body. Very uncomfortable.

"Besides," said Jessie. "I already have a lesson I'm going to teach her. And everyone in the class will be in on it."

David's face brightened. "Good! I knew you would think of something. You always have ideas. You know, Jessie, you're the smartest person I know."

Jessie couldn't help smiling at *that*. She liked it when people noticed she was smart. She liked it when people noticed her in almost any way. Sometimes it was hard to get attention with a big brother like Evan. He was popular and friendly, so lots of times he was the center of attention and Jessie felt left in a corner and forgotten. Maybe it was because she was so small. But then she perked up thinking about how being small was going to help her win the bridge-building contest. She certainly couldn't have crossed the bridge if she was as big as Evan.

"So, what are we going to do to her?" asked David eagerly. "Ruin something of hers? We should staple shut her backpack. Or spill glitter glue all over her shoes. She loves her shoes!"

Jessie made a face at David. "You'll see what lesson we're going to teach her *later*. And everyone in the class will be a part of it."

"The last day of camp!" said David. "That's perfect. She won't have time to do anything to get back at us."

"David," said Jessie. "I need to work on my bridge, and you are really annoying me right now. Can you go help Katrina with her troll bridge? She wants to add blinking lights."

"Sure," said David, who knew Jessie well enough not to be offended. He headed over to the other art table and began cutting sparkle string for Katrina's suspension cables.

A little later, Jessie looked up from her bridge to see Becky standing in front of her. She had her arms folded across her chest, and she looked like she would rather be anywhere in the world—including buried up to her neck in an anthill—than standing in front of Jessie.

"What do you want?" asked Jessie.

"Nothing!" said Becky.

Jessie shrugged and went back to reinforcing her bridge with extra Popsicle sticks.

"Only my mom wants to take a picture of your dumb bridge," Becky said. "For the town newspaper. You know, the one that gets delivered for free on Thursdays."

Jessie knew that paper! She and Evan had had their picture in it last summer when they won the Labor Day contest by selling lemonade to raise money for charity.

"She takes pictures for lots of papers, and when I complained to her about how you were ruining the class because of this stupid contest, she said it would be a great local story. She wants to take the picture of you with your bridge outside and then pitch the story to the editor of the paper. He might not even want it!"

Jessie loved getting her picture in the paper. It had happened three times before, and she really wanted it to happen again. "Sure!" she said. "When?"

"It has to be tomorrow, because that's the only time my mom has."

"But the contest is tomorrow," said Jessie. "And it's a long drive."

"So, meet her in the morning. She gets up early. She told me to tell you that you should set up the bridge so that it crosses the stream on the playground. She says a picture like that has the best chance of getting the editor to say yes. It can't just be a boring picture of a kid standing next to a model bridge."

"Okay!" said Jessie with enthusiasm. "Evan and I can carry it outside this afternoon and then it'll be all set up for your mom to take the picture."

"Whatever," said Becky. Jessie could see how

much Becky hated giving this good news to Jessie.

Becky shifted her weight from one leg to the other. "I'm just the messenger. Don't blame me if it doesn't work out. You deal with it." Which Jessie thought was kind of an odd thing to say.

But who cared! She was going to be famous! In the town newspaper. Now everyone in town would recognize her and know how smart she was. Plus, they would all see her amazing bridge. She hurried to get back to work.

CHAPTER 16
SOMEONE
SMALLER

"You told!" shouted Reed.

"What?" Evan didn't usually stumble, but this time his legs got caught on the picnic table bench as he tried to stand up. Stevie had already gone into a semi-crouch position, now that his knights were safely hidden in his pocket. He huddled his back against the oncoming enemy, his head bent low over the top of the table.

"You and that puny sewer rat!" Reed shouted, pointing at Stevie. "You told the principal about what happened! You said it was my fault! You lousy . . . You're nothing but a . . ." And he let loose with a string of swear words that were so jumbled up, they didn't even make sense.

"I didn't," said Evan, still struggling to untangle his legs from the splintery bench. "I didn't tell anyone. And neither did Stevie."

"Liar. I'm going to make both of you sorry you were ever born. You hear that, Albert! I'm talking to *you!*"

Evan was directly between Reed and Stevie, who was now covering his head with both hands, ready for the attack. Reed was coming at Evan so fast that Evan thought he would knock him right off his feet. He looked like a high-speed train that couldn't be stopped.

But now Evan had gotten his legs under him. He was standing up straight, both feet planted on the ground.

There was no way he was going to let a coward like Reed take a swing at him. Or do anything to hurt Stevie.

Evan charged at him, head up and arms at his sides so that when they collided, he bumped Reed with his chest, hard enough that Reed was thrown back. Evan balled up his fists. Was *this* going to be his first fistfight? He didn't know how to do this, but his body seemed to take over, the way it did on the basketball court.

"His name is *Stevie!*" shouted Evan.

He charged at Reed again.

Reed took three steps back. Then two more.

"What are you, nuts?" shouted Reed. The look on Reed's face told Evan that no one had ever stood up to him before. Everyone he'd ever challenged had probably run away or curled up like Stevie. And now Reed didn't know what to do.

"Just leave us alone!" shouted Evan, advancing several more steps, which caused Reed to back up even more. His friends—Frank and Puke and Twitch—had scattered, disappearing into the crowd of kids. Evan could feel his heart pounding, as well as the coiled-up sensation in his legs he got when he was dribbling up-court against an aggressive defense. There was going to be body contact, but he felt bigger, taller than he was, the way he did when there was a mismatch and he would say inside his head, *I know I can take this guy.*

He started to run at Reed, waving his arms. "Get away from us! Get out of here! We're not afraid of you! Nobody's afraid of you, Reed!"

Reed backpedaled so fast, he half stumbled before catching himself, then shouted, "You are completely insane, you know that? I wouldn't get within ten feet of you if you paid me. Forget it! I am *out* of here!" Then he turned and headed for the school building. Over his shoulder, he shouted, "This isn't the end!"

But Evan was pretty sure it was. Reed would keep his distance.

Evan sat back down on the bench, breathing hard. Now that it was over, he had time to feel scared. Stevie was peering at him sideways, his shoulders still hunched, his body in a crouch.

"I wish I could do that," he said quietly.

Evan tried to slow his breathing down. For a wild

second, he thought he might cry; he had that feeling of tightness in his throat. But then he remembered he was out in the world, where everyone could see him, and he fought back the feeling.

"You could do that," said Evan. But he knew that wasn't true.

They sat quietly for a moment, Evan still going over in his head what had just happened. Had he really just attacked a kid on the playground? He'd never done that before. That's not who he was.

How was it that Reed was *still* making Evan feel like he wasn't himself?

When his breathing slowed to normal, Evan asked, "Stevie, how do you think the principal found out?"

Stevie shrugged. "Miss Dixon was on duty that day. I don't think she saw you, but she saw Reed and Frank. And, you know, sometimes teachers *know*."

"Why didn't you tell her it was me? That I was the one who did it?"

"Because it wasn't really you," said Stevie. "I

could tell. You looked more upset than me. And I was the one covered in goose turds."

There was a tense moment of silence, and then Evan and Stevie both burst out laughing.

"What do you think he'll do now?" asked Stevie.

"I don't know. He'll leave us alone, though," said Evan, hoping it was true.

"He'll leave *you* alone," said Stevie. "It might be worse for me. Or someone else. He'll probably pick on someone even smaller. That's what bullies do."

And Evan knew that was true. Bullies always figure out how to punch down. He'd find someone, somewhere who was smaller.

Evan wondered who that smaller person would be.

CHAPTER 17
HOW AN ARCH BRIDGE WORKS

Katrina was crying.

Jessie tried to block out the sound, but it was nearly impossible.

"I miss Pixie," Katrina managed to say between wails.

"We all do," said Lorelei.

Jessie sat up. She didn't like it when statements were made without facts to support them. Was it true? *Did* everybody miss Pixie?

"Let's take a vote," said Jessie. She looked around

the classroom. Mrs. Feeney was talking on the classroom telephone. She spent an awful lot of time doing that for someone who was supposed to be substitute teaching. But it was the last day of Summer Fun Exploration Camp, and both the kids and Mrs. Feeney seemed to have reached an agreement: They could do what they wanted as long as she could do what she wanted. Sadly, everyone had lost interest in making fairy houses. Without Pixie, there just didn't seem to be much point.

The kids, who had been slumping on their art stools with nothing to do, sat up and looked at Jessie. Everyone liked voting. It was a chance to come together. Or have an argument. Either way, it was more interesting than doing nothing.

"Who here misses Pixie?"

Five hands shot in the air. Actually six, because Katrina raised both.

Jessie had not raised her hand and neither had Becky. But Jessie was taking the time to think about something she hadn't thought about before. Did she *really* miss Pixie? Jessie made a list in her head.

Pixie was not a real grownup or a real teacher. She dressed in silly costumes when it wasn't Halloween. She read terrible stories that weren't even true, and she told lies about fairies, particularly to Katrina.

On the other hand, Pixie always said nice things about Jessie's fairy houses and her bridges, and Jessie liked getting compliments. Also, Pixie played the ukulele really well, and she had a pretty singing voice, even though it cracked on the highest notes. She had a friendly smile. She kept her hands clean, which was important to Jessie. And after that first time, she never tried to touch Jessie again, not even a light hand on her shoulder, which some people never seemed to understand, even when Jessie explained it *very carefully* to them. But Pixie had understood that part of Jessie right away, and so she saved all her hugs and snuggles for Katrina, who loved sitting on Pixie's lap during the Fairy Circle at the end of the day.

Most of all, though, Pixie had done her best. Doing your best mattered to Jessie. It was one of the reasons she got so angry at Mrs. Feeney, who never seemed to try at all. Mrs. Feeney was like a big, droopy white flag, constantly surrendering without a fight.

Yes. Jessie missed Pixie. She raised her hand.

That left only Becky, who still sat by herself at the far end of the last art table.

"I don't care," she said. "I *don't* miss her. She was a terrible teacher."

Teacher! That reminded Jessie of her plan. She was going to teach the whole class something really important about bridges. She had prepared yesterday at home for this best and final experiment.

"Well!" said Mrs. Feeney, hanging up the phone and turning her attention to the class. The students stared at her with expectant looks on their faces. Was she going to tell them what the phone call had been about? Would she direct them in an activity? Was there any news of Pixie?

"What's the plan for today?" she asked as she turned to look at Jessie.

It was a good thing Jessie had something in

mind. Otherwise, this Summer Fun Exploration Camp would go right off the rails!

"I'm going to show how an arch bridge works," Jessie said, leaving the art table with her finished bridge and standing at the front of the classroom. "And then we're all going to make an arch bridge together."

Quickly, she drew the same drawing on the whiteboard that she had shown Evan earlier. She told everyone about the ancient Romans, how they had invented a special kind of waterproof cement called *pozzolana* made from the ash that blew out of the Mount Vesuvius volcano, how they devised a way to build underwater using something called a *cofferdam*, how their bridges were still standing and cars and trucks passed over them every day, even though the bridges were more than two thousand years old.

All of this knowledge had been in her special book, *The Great Big Book of Bridges*, and even though the book was glued shut and could never be opened again, Jessie could still pass all of this important, scientific knowledge on to the students at camp. She was sad that her book was ruined, and she didn't understand why Becky had done it, but there was no way anyone could lock up the knowledge of bridge building. Even if her book was destroyed, Jessie still knew what made an arch bridge stay standing for thousands of years.

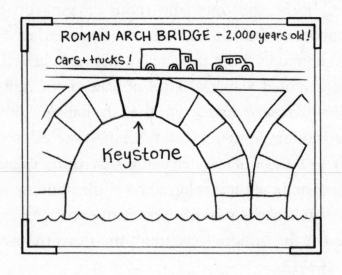

"That can't work!" said Andrea, looking at Jessie's diagram.

"It would fall apart," said David, moving his

hands into the shape of an arch then splitting them open. "Especially if those stones weigh eight tons each."

"It would totally collapse," said Lorelei.

"I believe Jessie!" said Katrina stubbornly. "Jessie always tells the truth."

"Thanks," said Jessie, looking at Katrina, "but I'm glad the rest of you have doubts. Because scientists never just believe what someone tells them. Scientists say, 'Prove it!' So I'm going to prove it to you."

She reached into her pockets and pulled out two handfuls of clay blocks. The blocks were all identical, and they looked just like the heavy Roman stones in the drawing, but much smaller. Jessie gave two blocks to each kid. The blocks were just big enough to hold securely between a thumb and an index finger.

Katrina immediately started to click her clay blocks together. "They're a funny shape!" she said.

"They remind me of something," said David, looking at Jessie. "What is it they look like?"

Jessie rolled her eyes. Some people were no good at remembering shapes and patterns.

"Here's how we're going to do it," she said. "I've taped these two pencils to the table. These are the abutments—"

Ava shrieked. "Jessie said 'butt'!"

"I did *not*," said Jessie, but everyone was laughing now, and Jessie had to wait thirty whole seconds until they settled down. "I'm going to say that word again, and anyone who laughs has to go wait out in the hall while the rest of us build a Roman arch bridge. Got it?" Jessie was small, but she could get people's attention when she wanted to.

"So, the pencils are like the *abutments*," she said loudly. Ava wriggled madly on her stool, but didn't laugh. "And that's the part of the bridge that's buried deep in the ground and holds everything steady. Now, who's going to be the first to put down a block next to the pencil?"

"Me! Me! Me!" shouted Katrina, bouncing so hard that she slipped off her stool.

The older kids didn't mind Katrina going first.

Jessie showed her how to line up her block in just the right spot. "Hold it there. Don't jiggle it. You have to keep it exactly where it is. Who wants to go next?"

And so, one by one, each student positioned two blocks in the growing arch that Jessie had designed. The bridge grew taller and rounder. It looked just like the picture in Jessie's book, the book that was ruined forever, the book that Becky had destroyed.

"There's a hole!" said Katrina, dismayed. They were all holding their blocks in place, hands criss-crossing over each other and trembling just a little with the effort of keeping everything where it was supposed to be. But Katrina was right: there was a gap at the top, like a missing tooth. It was the size of one block.

"Yep," said Jessie, struggling to hold her own blocks in place. "We need one more."

"Do you have one?" asked Andrea. "Because this is really getting hard to hold."

"Of course, I do," said Jessie. "It's the keystone, and it's in my pocket. But I can't get it because I can't let go of my blocks!"

No one else could either. Everyone was desperately trying to hold their bridge blocks in place. Mrs. Feeney was back on the phone, her back turned to them.

"Becky, help us!" said Katrina. "We need you to put the keystone on top!"

"I'm not helping with any dumb bridge," said Becky.

"C'mon, Becky," said David. And then a chorus of cries rang out: "Yeah, Becky!" "Help us out." "We need a hand. Like, seriously!"

"Please," said Jessie. She had planned for this moment, and she really wanted it to work, but Jessie wasn't good at guessing what other people would do.

Becky made a big show of getting up from her seat and slowly walking over to the art table where all the students were clustered. Everyone started to cheer. "Becky! Becky! Becky!" and that made Becky laugh in a sort of self-conscious way.

"Stop it!" she said. "You're all acting like dorks." But she smiled again.

Jessie said, "See the chain hanging out of my

pocket? Just pull on it, and the keystone is on the end."

Becky looked at the thin silver chain dangling delicately from Jessie's pants pocket, and her eyes grew wide. "I can take it?" she asked.

"Yes," said Jessie. "It's yours anyway. It was a gift from your grandparents. That means it's yours forever. I really just wanted it to teach you a lesson. I mean, this lesson. About the Roman arch bridge."

Becky tugged the chain out of Jessie's pocket and the beautiful rose quartz pendant swung hypnotically on the end of it.

"It's so beautiful," said Katrina in a whisper. "The most rarest stone of all."

"It is not!" said Jessie. "Quartz is very common! That's a fact! But it doesn't matter, because we don't need a rare stone right now. We just need a keystone. And that's what it is." She directed Becky to use the necklace chain like a crane to lower the keystone into place, and when it was perfectly positioned, she told everyone to let go of their clay blocks.

"No!" said Katrina. "It will all fall! The bridge won't stand up if we don't hold it."

"Yes, it will," said Jessie firmly.

"Are you sure?" asked David.

"We'll never know unless we try," said Jessie.

Slowly all six students let go of their blocks. Katrina was the last to let go.

The bridge stood. The keystone held everything in place.

"You see," said Jessie. "It's science." And science was better than any fairy tale. But it was also a little magical.

They all marveled at the bridge they'd made, and then David got the idea of how to bust it up, which is always the most fun of building anything from blocks. "Hey, Becky!" he said. "Pull the keystone out of the top. Like a cork out of a bottle!"

"Should I?" asked Becky, still holding the dangling silver chain in her hand.

"Sure," said Jessie. "We can always build it again if we want."

"Do it! Do it!" shouted the other kids.

"Wait!" shouted Katrina. She ran to get her trolls so that they could watch the bridge come tumbling down too.

As soon as Becky pulled out the keystone, the whole bridge collapsed. Everyone clapped, which brought Mrs. Feeney over to the table. She took one look at the pile of clay blocks on the table and shook her head. "I really don't get kids these days." Then she wandered back to her desk and left them in peace to build and rebuild the bridge. It was Katrina who had the idea to paint the clay blocks, so that took up the rest of the morning right up until the lunch break.

Jessie was happy. The whole room felt lighter. She realized that as much as she had wanted Becky to stop being mean to *her*, she had wanted to stop being mean to Becky, too. Maybe even more. And taking the necklace had been mean. Sometimes it feels good to get back at someone who's hurt you. But that doesn't always make you feel better in the end. Sometimes it takes something more to heal old wounds.

Becky wandered over to Jessie, who was taking her lunch box out of her cubby. "Jessie," said Becky, "I have to tell you something."

Jessie looked at Becky's face, but she couldn't read it at all. The closest she could figure was that Becky had eaten something that was giving her a very bad stomachache. But they hadn't even gone to lunch yet, so that didn't seem to make sense.

"My mom can't take the photo tomorrow," said Becky. "She's got something else she needs to do."

"What does she need to do?" asked Jessie.

"I . . . I don't remember," said Becky. "Something, she said. And she asked me to tell you."

"Why didn't you tell me before?" asked Jessie. "You waited all morning. Why?"

"I didn't . . . it's not that long that I waited. I forgot about it . . . and then . . . well, we did the bridge thing . . . and you gave me back my necklace . . ." Becky's face was slowly turning a deep crimson.

Jessie noticed the color rise from her neck and creep up her cheeks. It was like a sunset in reverse.

"Why are you so red?" asked Jessie. She didn't understand at all what was going on. How could Becky's mother change her mind? When Jessie's mother made a promise, she stuck to it. Or had a good reason not to.

Becky's hands flew up to her cheeks, as if by covering them she could make the red disappear. "I'm not red! And I'm telling you now. What does it matter when I tell you? She can't do it. So, you don't need to take the bridge to the stream this afternoon."

"But we're *all* going to do that!" said Katrina loudly. "It was going to be like a parade. And Jessie said I could lead the way with my trolls!" She held up the trolls, one in each hand, as if they were as disappointed as she was.

"It's not my fault!" said Becky, her voice rising. "It wasn't my idea in the first place . . . and I always get stuck in the middle like this. It isn't fair!"

By now, all the students in the camp class had gathered around their cubbies and were listening to the drama in the hallway. Jessie looked at David to see if he understood what was going on, but he had a strange look on his face that seemed to say he was as puzzled as Jessie. Becky's face was still bright red, and she looked like her stomachache had reached the point when something might actually come up.

"Are you doing this to be mean to me?" asked Jessie.

"I am *not* being mean." Becky turned to look at all the other students who were staring at her, with her red face and stammering answers that sounded like lies. "I'm not mean. And this isn't fair." She pulled her own lunch box down from the shelf and said in a sharp voice that sounded like little fire-crackers exploding, "Fine. I'll tell my mother to change her plans. She'll meet you at the bridge by the stream and take your picture. Happy?"

Katrina cheered and then danced with her trolls, one in each hand. Becky pushed past Jessie and returned to the classroom. David walked over.

"What do you think *that* was about?" he asked Jessie.

"I don't know. All I care is that I get to have my picture in the paper." Jessie smiled. She would send a copy to her father.

"I think she made up the part about her mom not being able to take the picture. I bet it makes her mad that her mom is paying attention to you. I guess she still doesn't like you."

Jessie shrugged. "I didn't understand Becky when we were in second grade, and I don't understand her now. I guess that's just the way it is with some people."

"I don't know," said David. "There's just something strange about her making up that story."

Lies. Jessie really didn't like them. As far as she was concerned, there was no good reason to tell a lie. She would talk to Evan when she got home. Maybe he could explain why Becky was still being mean to her even after Jessie gave her back the keystone necklace.

CHAPTER 18
FRIDAY #3

Three weeks of summer school—done! Evan dropped his backpack in the hall and went into the kitchen to get a snack.

Three done, but five more to go. Still, after today, he figured the rest of summer school would be a little bit better. And he noticed that the strange feeling he'd had—that feeling of not really being himself—had mostly disappeared.

"Evan!" Jessie's voice was sharp, but Evan was

used to that. He knew it just meant she was focused on something.

"What?"

"You're on time!"

"Yep!" said Evan, heading straight for the refrigerator and grabbing some string cheese. "And my shoelaces are tied!" He laughed. Jessie wouldn't understand, but he knew what he meant.

"You have to wash your hands when you get home. And before you eat. That's a double hand-washing situation."

"I was going to!" said Evan. "You don't have to tell me everything I need to do, Jessie."

"But I need to tell you *some* things, and I can't always tell what the *some* things are and what they're not. Like right now, I need to tell you that you have to help me carry my model bridge to the stream."

"I thought you were having a parade to do that," said Evan.

"Mrs. Feeney wouldn't let us! She said it counted as a field trip, and there was no way she was going to make the effort to get permission for a field trip on the last day of Summer Fun Exploration Camp. She is the worst teacher *ever!*"

Evan had had Mrs. Feeney as a sub many times over his years at Hillside, and he agreed with Jessie completely.

"Let me finish my snack and say hi to Mom, and then we can go," he said.

"And you're coming to the bridge-building contest tomorrow, right?"

"Sure," he said. He knew how much the contest meant to Jessie. She'd hardly talked about anything else since summer vacation began. Plus, he didn't want his mom and Jessie carrying the model bridge from the parking lot to the building where the contest was being held. Jessie might drop it. Even his mom might trip carrying that thing. It was *huge*.

As Evan and Jessie walked to Hillside Elementary School, Jessie told him all about the strange way Becky had behaved that afternoon at Summer Fun Exploration Camp. Then she started asking him questions, the way she always did when she didn't understand why people said certain things or why they acted in certain ways. Jessie was the smartest person Evan knew, but she could be clueless when it came to people.

"Why did she first say her mother *couldn't* take the picture, then say her mother *could?*" asked Jessie.

"I don't know," said Evan.

"But she was definitely lying, right?"

"It sounds like it," said Evan. "Maybe she wanted to do something else with her mom on Saturday morning, but her mom can't because of the photo, so she told you her mom had to cancel. Or maybe her mom's not feeling well, and she wanted to let her mom sleep in so she'd feel better." Evan often tried to do things to make his mom's life easier. He knew how hard she worked to be a good parent *and* to earn enough money for all the things they needed. Evan liked to help when he could.

When they turned the corner and the school was in sight, Jessie asked, "Are you back to normal?"

"What?" asked Evan.

"You've been really weird. For days! Even Mom noticed."

"Has she been worried?" asked Evan, but he already knew the answer.

"Yes," said Jessie. "And she asked *me* about it." Both Evan and Jessie tried not to worry their mom. It was a promise they had made years ago when their father left.

"Sorry, I've been acting weird," said Evan. "I haven't felt like myself since I started summer school."

"That doesn't make any sense," said Jessie. "You *are* yourself and so that means you have to *feel* like yourself, because however you're feeling, that's yourself. And you feel like it. *QED*."

Evan laughed and put his hand up for their own special high five—both of them raising their palms and swinging them past each other without touching. Jessie liked to use grown-up words like *QED*, which just means "There's the proof of what I just said." And Jessie liked to *prove* things and then tell you that she had proved it. Having a sister like Jessie was . . . never boring.

"But now you're back to normal?" asked Jessie again.

"Yep!" he said. "Shoelaces tied and everything!"

"Good, because I don't like having a brother who's acting weird," said Jessie.

"That doesn't make sense," said Evan, smiling. "Because you like having me as your brother, and I've been acting weird, so that means you like having a brother who's acting weird. *QED*."

"Stop it," said Jessie. "We have work to do."

Evan pulled open the front door of the school and they both stepped inside. He'd been going to this elementary school since he was a kindergartener, and now he was going to be a fifth-grader— his last year here before going to the middle school for good. In that moment, he wished he could stay here forever.

CHAPTER 19
AN UNEXPECTED VISITOR

On Saturday morning, Jessie was up early, even for her. She was butterfly-stomach excited: eager for the contest, but worried that the bridge wouldn't hold her weight as planned. Luckily, she would have the chance to test it this morning when Becky's mother took the photo for the town newspaper.

Evan had encouraged her to test it yesterday after they'd positioned it over the stream, but Jessie had refused. "If I test it now and it breaks, then there won't be a photo in the newspaper. But if

Becky's mom takes the photo with me standing *next* to the bridge, then I'll get my picture in the paper. And *then* I can test it before the contest." Jessie liked to think at least three steps ahead. It made her feel calm to know that she had figured out every possible option in a situation. No unexpected outcomes.

But she wasn't feeling calm this morning, because she was so excited to get her picture taken. She wasn't even worrying about the contest! She just wanted to show everyone how wonderful her suspension bridge was. And that it was a *real* bridge, one that could actually carry a person over a stream. She hoped.

Her jumping stomach wasn't in much of a mood for any breakfast, but Jessie knew that a bowl of cereal would settle her down. She crept downstairs. It was so early, the whole neighborhood was still asleep. Only the summer sun was up, and Jessie felt a wonderful sense of all the possibilities that the day held.

She had finished half the bowl of cereal when

she heard a light knocking on the door. At first, Jessie wondered if it was a bird pecking at a tree outside, but it came again and then again.

Jessie tiptoed to the front door and said, "Who is it?" She wasn't going to open the door without first knowing who was out there. It could be anyone!

"It's Becky," whispered a voice.

Jessie opened the door. "What are you doing here? It's way too early for people to knock on people's doors."

"I had to tell you something and I have to tell you now, because in half an hour it's going to be too late." Becky looked like she'd been crying, and her face was starting to crumple up in that way that told Jessie she might start crying again. "Can I come in?"

Jessie frowned. This was all very strange. She didn't trust Becky. This girl had been mean to her and had told her things that weren't true. And Jessie wasn't supposed to have friends over to the house without her mother's permission. Jessie felt her butterfly stomach do a butterfly leap.

"Please?" said Becky.

"Okay," said Jessie. She hoped her mother wouldn't be mad if she found out. And she hoped this wasn't a mean trick that Becky was playing on her. Jessie let Becky into the front hall, but kept the door open, in case.

"My mother isn't taking your photo for the school paper," said Becky.

"Again?" said Jessie, exasperated. This was ridiculous. "But the bridge is already in place."

"I *know!*" said Becky, getting louder. "That was the whole point!"

"Be quiet! Be quiet!" said Jessie, not at all quietly. "Everyone's sleeping. It's Saturday."

"My brother is going to destroy your bridge. My mother doesn't even know you built a bridge because I never told her. I told my brother . . . and . . . and I told him I was really mad at you, because you'd taken my necklace away . . . and he said we should play a joke on you and trick you into putting your bridge outside . . . and then he was going to break it."

"What? Why?" asked Jessie, her heart beating loudly in her ears.

"Because he said it would teach you a lesson about not taking things from people."

"But I won it, fair and square!" said Jessie. She knew this wasn't the point, but her brain couldn't make sense of why Becky and her brother wanted to be so mean to her. It wasn't logical. There was no way to reach *QED* when it came to proving why Becky hated her so much.

"I'm sorry!" said Becky, her eyes starting to leak.

"My bridge!" said Jessie. "We have to save it!"

"I can't! I can't!" said Becky, and now she was really crying. "My brother will kill me, he'll be so mad I told you. I can't go with you."

"You *have* to go with me," said Jessie. "This is your fault too, not just your brother's."

"I can't!"

Evan. Jessie needed Evan. "I'm going to get my brother. Wait here. Don't move. I'll be back in one minute."

Jessie was glad she was already dressed. She didn't even knock on Evan's bedroom door. It was slightly open anyway. When she walked in, she saw that Evan's bed was empty.

Where was Evan this early in the morning? He never got up early. Evan stayed up later than Jessie at night and usually woke up an hour after she did. Where could he be?

There was no time to figure it out. Jessie had to save her bridge. She and Becky would stand up to Becky's brother. She wished that Evan was at her side too, but she knew that she and Becky could save the bridge. Together.

But when Jessie went downstairs, Becky was gone. The hallway was empty. The front door was still open, and Becky was nowhere to be seen.

Jessie yanked on her sneakers and tied the laces with double knots, the way she always did. Then she hurried out the door and ran the six blocks to school. Leaving the house without her mom's permission was definitely not allowed, but Jessie had no choice. She had worked too long and too hard on her bridge to let some mean boy she'd never even heard of ruin it for no good reason.

She ran across the field toward the bridge, then she stopped. Jessie scanned the school playground for any sign of an older boy. It was so quiet, Jessie could hear the murmuring sound of the tall grass and the quiet rippling of the small stream. She even thought she could hear the slight crackling sound of the geese turning and resettling on their nests.

As she got closer, she could see that the bridge was exactly where she had left it. But someone had made a mess on it. There was a small pile of leaves and dried grass on the deck, as if a young child had been throwing things in the air and they had landed on the bridge.

Jessie stopped and stood still, listening. She didn't see another human.

Until she did.

About twenty feet away from the bridge, hidden by the tall grass, something moved. Jessie looked closely, and she could just barely make out the tops of two heads. The faces were hidden.

"I see you!" shrieked Jessie. "You stay away!" Then she charged forward to put herself between Becky's brother and her bridge.

CHAPTER 20
THE BRIDGE BETWEEN

"Who *is* that?" asked Stevie.

"Holy crud! It's my sister!" Evan leaped to his feet. "Shhh! Shhh!" he said urgently, pressing his arms downward to signal to Jessie that she should be quiet.

What was Jessie doing here? Stevie had told Evan late last night about Reed's plan to destroy the bridge, long after Jessie had gone to bed. And Jessie hadn't been awake when Evan left the house early to meet Stevie to defend the bridge. Evan was still hoping in his heart that Reed wouldn't show and the photo would go as planned.

"Evan!" said Jessie. "I tried to wake you up, but you weren't in bed! Why weren't you in bed?"

"Because Stevie told me that Reed was going to try to destroy your bridge."

"No," said Jessie. "*Not* Reed. Becky's brother. That's who's going to break the bridge."

"No, *Reed*," said Evan. "Stevie overheard him yesterday talking about it. But Stevie didn't figure out it was *you* until he remembered me telling him about your contest."

Jessie turned to Stevie. "You must not have heard right," she said. "It's definitely Becky's brother. She told me."

"No, it's Reed," said Stevie. "I didn't hear everything, but I know it was Reed."

Jessie shook her head. "It's Becky's brother."

Evan and Jessie looked at each other.

"No way," said Evan.

Jessie put her hands on her head as if she was afraid it would explode.

Reed, the kid who had been tormenting Evan all summer, was Becky's brother? Becky, the girl who had been bullying Jessie since second grade, was Reed's sister?

"What a family," said Stevie.

That stopped Evan. He had never thought about that. Reed had a family. What would it be like to wake up every morning and share the same toothpaste tube with Reed? Eat breakfast with Reed. Watch TV with Reed. Pass him on the stairs, where he could push you or trip you or shove you. What would it be like to never be able to get away from Reed?

"Becky was crying this morning," said Jessie. "She was *scared*. She ran away."

"There he is," said Stevie. Evan could tell that Stevie was trying to sound brave, but he didn't. Evan felt his own heart start to speed up. He was suddenly aware that he was responsible for Stevie *and* Jessie. They were smaller than he was. He didn't have to protect just the bridge; he had to protect them.

It felt like too much.

Reed was walking in that strange bouncing way he had. Evan realized he used it to make himself look bigger than he was. Like he was taking up more space. Like he was confident.

Evan knew he wasn't. But Evan wasn't feeling so confident either.

Reed was coming at the bridge from the side of the middle school. Evan, Jessie, and Stevie were on the side of the bridge closest to Hillside Elementary. The four-foot-wide stream was between them. The bridge was the only way over.

Evan suddenly remembered what Stevie had said the last time Evan confronted Reed: *He'll probably pick on someone even smaller.*

It had never occurred to Evan that it would be Jessie.

"You two should go," said Evan. "I'll take care of this."

"No," said Stevie. "I'm going to stay."

"Jessie, go home," said Evan. Reed was getting closer, and he wasn't slowing down at all.

"Are you crazy?" asked Jessie. "It's *my* bridge. You're not the boss of me, Evan Treski."

"Besides," said Stevie, "there are three of us. That has to count for something."

Evan wasn't so sure. Reed was almost at the stream and he still hadn't slowed down. It looked to Evan like he had a plan.

"Hey!" shouted Reed. "What are *you* doing, Goose Boy? Babysitting?"

Evan advanced. "Get out of here, Reed."

Reed laughed. "You're going to make me?"

Evan saw how Reed had him caught. The stream was Reed's extra weapon. It kept him safe from Evan, but it didn't protect the bridge. And Evan couldn't cross the bridge without destroying it.

Reed took a deliberate step.

Evan turned to Jessie. "Run and get Mom."

"There isn't time!" said Jessie. "He'll ruin it before she gets here. I'm not leaving!"

"Stevie," said Evan. "Run up the hill and get someone. Tell someone."

"She's right," said Stevie. "He'll smash it and be gone before anyone comes."

Reed took another deliberate step toward the bridge. He was grinning. Evan could tell that this was his idea of fun.

Evan advanced a few steps. The slow, murky water was in front of him. Ever since he was a kindergartener, he'd been told to *stay out of the water*. He thought about the snakes under the surface and other stories the kids told of bloodsucking leeches and parasites.

Reed laughed. He picked up one of the heavy rocks that Evan and Jessie had used to anchor the bridge on each side.

And now Evan realized what Reed had already figured out: Even if Evan did plunge into the snake-filled water to defend the bridge, he wouldn't reach Reed in time. All Reed had to do was heave that one heavy rock onto the center of the bridge, and the whole thing would splinter to pieces.

"Evan! *E-van!*" cried Jessie. Evan couldn't bear the anguish in her voice. It reminded him how she'd cried when their father left.

There was nothing he could do to protect her.

Suddenly, there was a loud noise across the water. A large Canada goose stepped out of the grass. It stretched itself to its full height, standing tall with its wings spread wide. Then it thrust its head forward, stuck out its long pink tongue, and began to hiss at Reed. Evan had never seen a bird that looked so huge. It was much bigger than Jessie.

The goose took a step toward Reed, bobbing its snakelike neck and hissing loudly, its pink tongue extending far out of its beak. Then it took another step. Reed stayed rooted to where he stood, weighed down by the stone and confused.

A second goose, slightly smaller, stepped out of the grass and did the same thing, stretching its neck up to the sky so that it stood tall like the mast of a ship with two broad sails unfurled on either side. It hissed just as loudly as the first one.

Stevie, Evan, and Jessie instinctively started to back away. Reed, however, seemed to decide to challenge the goose. He lifted the heavy rock, as if he might throw it at the bird, and shouted, *"Heya*, get out of here!"

Both geese dropped their heads low to the ground, tucked their wings tight to their bodies, and charged at Reed with astonishing speed. It was like watching a bicycle rocketing downhill. When the geese reached Reed, they spread their wings and flew up off the ground, extending their long necks and pecking his head with their bills.

Reed tried to drop the rock and turn, but he tripped and stumbled. He was on the ground, with the two birds swirling around him, flying up into the air and pecking his body, all the while hissing loudly. Flying and pecking, then landing and hissing.

"Evan!" shouted Jessie. "They're going to peck him to death!"

Evan started to run toward the water. Snakes or no snakes, he had to do something.

But before he reached the edge, Reed struggled to his feet and ran away, screaming as if his pants were on fire. As soon as he took off, the pair of geese settled down and began walking in gentle circles, calming themselves and nibbling the grass quietly.

"Whoa!" said Stevie. "I've never seen anything like that!"

"Do you think they'll come over here?" asked Jessie, who had taken ahold of the back of Evan's T-shirt. It was the closest she came to holding hands with anyone.

"I don't think they care about us," said Evan, breathing heavily, sweat dripping off his forehead.

"Why did they do that?" asked Stevie. "Why'd they attack Reed, and now they're just walking around like nothing happened?"

"It's a well-known fact that geese will attack humans when they're threatened," said Jessie. "Or their babies are threatened. Or their nest is threatened."

"I don't see any babies," said Evan. "And I think that's the pair of geese with the nest that Reed smashed."

"Look at that," said Stevie. Evan and Jessie watched as the geese ripped mouthfuls of grass from the ground and carried them to the bridge. They waddled onto the bridge as if they had done this before and deposited the grass in the middle of the deck.

"They're dumping stuff on my bridge!" said Jessie. "They can't do that. I want it clean for the contest."

"Jess," said Evan slowly. "I think they're building another nest."

"No!" said Jessie. "I refuse to give them permission to build a nest on my bridge."

"I think they're already doing it," said Stevie. He was smiling. Evan started to smile too.

"You have to admit, Jess," said Evan. "It's pretty cool. Out of all the places they could have built a nest, they chose your bridge. It's *kind of* like winning a contest."

"It's nothing like winning a contest," said Jessie. There would be no ribbon to hang on her wall. No photo in the newspaper. No applause. "I want my bridge back now!"

"Well, go get it," said Stevie, stepping back.

"Yeah," said Evan, taking two steps back. "There's no way I'm going to fight with those geese!"

"This is awful!" said Jessie.

"No, it's great," said Evan. "They lost their first nest, and now you've given them a home for their second one. You're one in a million, Jess. I bet they name a goose baby after you!"

"Gosling!" said Jessie with frustration. "A goose baby is called a gosling!"

"I bet you *will* get your picture in the paper," said Stevie. "Who else has built a bridge out of Popsicle sticks that's strong enough to hold a goose and a nest?"

Jessie hadn't thought of that. "I suppose it is newsworthy." She looked at the nest. "Oh, no! Did that goose poop near my bridge?" She turned and started to walk away. "There is no way I'm taking that bridge back. Goose poop! Yuck!"

CHAPTER 21
APPLAUSE

Jessie handed the binoculars to Pixie and continued to draw in her nature notebook. "They have five eggs so far. But the female might keep laying. Canada geese typically have egg clutches of two to nine eggs."

Jessie, Pixie, and Evan were lying on their stomachs watching the nest. They knew to keep their distance. That's why they had the binoculars.

"I'm glad I get to see it in person," said Pixie. "The picture in the paper was too small."

"I know!" said Jessie indignantly. She thought the picture should have been on page one, but instead it was on page twelve. At least the reporter wrote a nice long article about her and spelled her name right. That was important too.

"Jessie told me you're in summer school," said Pixie, handing the binoculars to Evan. "I did summer school a couple of times. It was hard to be in class when all my friends were having fun."

"Yeah," said Evan, "but I'm halfway through." He didn't add, *And Reed stopped coming*. Reed hadn't shown up for class on Monday, and he'd been absent every day since then. Evan didn't know why, and he didn't ask.

"It helped me," said Pixie. She stretched out Superman-style in the dry summer grass and pulled up a tiny weed with a purple flower on it. "Do you think it's helping you?"

"Definitely." Evan nodded. "It's okay. I'm teaching a friend to play basketball. Well, H-O-R-S-E, not really basketball. He's pretty small."

"That's nice," said Pixie. "I bet you're a good teacher, like Jessie."

"I'm the best teacher because I teach things that are real," said Jessie, taking the binoculars from Evan. She liked looking at the geese from a safe distance. It was like being a scientist in the field. Plus, she didn't have to get near the goose poop.

"Well," said Pixie. "It was really nice that you organized all the kids from class to come to my house."

"I like to organize," said Jessie.

"It meant a lot to me. And it meant a lot to my mom that you all thought I was a good teacher, even if Mrs. Richter didn't."

"Oh, forget Mrs. Richter! What does she know? You're the best teacher of unreal things I ever knew. You should teach something real, like science or math."

Pixie laughed, and Jessie remembered how much she liked Pixie's laugh. "I'm just going to concentrate on finishing college," said Pixie. "That's enough for me."

"And I'm just going to concentrate on finishing summer school," said Evan. "That's enough for me."

Jessie, still looking at the geese through the binoculars, tried to think about what would be enough for her. Not so long ago, she had thought it would be enough if only she could win the bridge-building contest. That wasn't going to happen! In fact, when she realized she couldn't even *enter* the contest, she'd thrown away all her work: her sketches, her calculations, her model bridges. What good were they now? There were geese living on her bridge, and *they* weren't going to give her a blue ribbon. They weren't going to give her anything for all her hard work.

To make matters worse, the next day David K. had shown her an article he'd found on the internet in which a very famous theoretical physicist who was also a professor at Dartmouth College argued that fairies absolutely exist in *some* universe, even if they might not exist in ours. She had not liked that article. The professor was a scientist. He said that fairies existed. Jessie felt very mixed up by this mixing-up of science and magic.

But then a thought occurred to her as she watched the geese walk side by side along her bridge. Things *can* exist side by side. There was something magic-like about the way a baby bird could peck its way out of a shell and find the whole world waiting on the other side. Just as there was something magic-like about the way an arch bridge could stand for thousands of years without anything holding it together. Maybe there was enough room in the universe for both science and magic. It was a difficult thought for Jessie, and she returned to looking at her bridge for reassurance.

Wait! What was that? A flash of magenta. A sparkle of light.

Jessie focused the binoculars closely on the space underneath the bridge.

Katrina's trolls! One on each side. Their arms uplifted, protecting the geese and her bridge. Jessie felt a great wave of happiness that they were there, just where they belonged.

One of the geese honked loudly and beat its wings together three times.

"Applause!" shouted Jessie with glee. And that was enough for her.

Books in the
LEMONADE WAR SERIES
by Jacqueline Davies

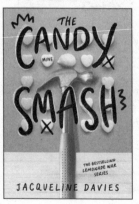

CLARION BOOKS

harpercollinschildrens.com